Wesley James Ruined My LIFE

Wesley James

James

Ruined My

LIFE

jennifer honeybourn

Swoon READS
Swoon Reads | NEW YORK

A SWOON READS BOOK

An Imprint of Feiwel and Friends and Macmillan Publishing Group LLC

Our books may be purchased in bulk for promotional, educational, or business use.
Please contact your local bookseller or the Macmillan Corporate and
Premium Sales Department at (800) 221-7945 ext. 5442 or by e-mail at
MacmillanSpecialMarkets@macmillan.com.

Library of Congress Cataloging-in-Publication Data is available.

ISBN 978-1-250-12373-2 (trade paperback) / ISBN 978-1-250-12374-9 (ebook)

Cover photo credits: Food truck © Maica/Getty Images; Frustrated girl and
boy © izusek/iStock by Getty Images; Stone patio © pics721/Shutterstock;
Crown doodle © LHF Graphics/Shutterstock; Cafe table and chair © guysal/
Shutterstock; Flowers in pot © Neirfy/Shutterstock; Union Jack flag © mickyteam/
Shutterstock; Heart pattern © Anastasiia Gevko/Shutterstock

First Edition—2017

1 3 5 7 9 10 8 6 4 2

swoonreads.com

FOR TONY AND LILA

 one.

King Henry VIII won't shut up.

Not the real King Henry VIII, obviously. That would be crazy, given the dude's been dead for five hundred years. This King Henry is really Alan Rickles, retired weatherman/local dinner theater actor.

He's been talking to me for the past five minutes, although it should be clear from the platters of food I'm holding that I'm on my way to a table. My arms ache from trying to keep the heavy silver trays balanced—each one is weighted down with a rapidly cooling turkey leg, tiny potatoes, and butter-glazed carrots, long green stems still attached. All of which our customers are invited to enjoy with their fingers instead of silverware, because knives and forks weren't used in the sixteenth century. At least not in King Henry's court.

"Anne. Everyone always blames me for what happened to Anne," Alan says, sighing. "That's all anyone remembers me for."

Of course that's what we remember him for. Henry had two of his wives beheaded. Not something people easily forget, even centuries later.

"What about all the good I did for England?" Alan strokes his thick brown beard. I'm convinced it's the reason he got the gig in the first place. That and the thirty extra pounds he gained for the role.

Yes. Alan gained thirty pounds to play King Henry VIII in a medieval theme restaurant in a strip mall outside of Seattle. Although I have to admit, in his fur-trimmed cape, heavily embroidered red tunic, and black velvet hat, he does look an awful lot like the portrait of Henry in my history textbook.

"I founded the Royal Navy, but do I get credit for that?" He shakes his head sadly. "No one remembers the good stuff."

My wrists start to shake. I adjust the platters so the food doesn't slide off, hoping Alan will finally get the hint and let me go. I can't walk away from him—we're supposed to stay in character while out on the restaurant floor, and servants don't walk away from kings. Not if they want to keep their heads, anyway.

And I don't want to make an enemy of Alan. He's really into using his royal position to send the junior staff to the stocks, this vaguely fencelike contraption used as a torture device in the Dark Ages. Now employed in our restaurant for entertainment purposes.

Basically, you stick your head and hands through these holes cut in the wooden boards and then the boards clap down, trapping you. There's no lock, for liability reasons, but God help you if you try to get out before Alan has granted you a pardon.

Looking around in increasing desperation—seriously, my wrists are going to snap off—I spot Joe, my boss, standing near the stage. He's talking to a guy dressed as a pirate. People sometimes come here dressed in their sixteenth-century finest, so at first I think it's just a customer channeling his inner Captain Jack Sparrow. But then I notice the pirate is carrying the staff orientation manual. The manual is filled with strict instructions on dress code, suggested old-timey hairstyles, and medieval words and phrases we're meant to pepper our conversations with, like *I bid you*, *fare thee well*, and, my personal favorite, *fie*—what passed for a swear word back in King Henry's time.

I'm too far away to tell what New Guy looks like—his face is partially obscured by an eye patch and the skull and crossbones hat—but I'm hoping he's cute. We are in desperate need of some cute around here.

"Did I ever tell you about the time I was grievously injured in a jousting accident?" Alan leans on his gold-tipped walking stick. It's the posture he adopts whenever he's settling in to tell a long, drawn-out tale.

I nod, but I can't help looking over his shoulder at New Guy. Joe jabs a stubby finger at the stage, no doubt telling him not to go anywhere near it. I remember getting the same speech when I first started three months ago. Unless we are needed for a skit, something that thankfully doesn't happen very often, no one but Alan and Julia, the woman who plays Catherine of Aragon, are allowed on the stage.

The set consists of a tall red velvet throne placed in front of silver swag curtains. Alan spends most of his time sitting on that throne, quietly surveying the audience. Except, of course, when he's on the restaurant floor, trying to convince whoever is in earshot that Henry VIII got a bum rap and was simply misunderstood.

I'm hoping Joe will notice Alan has me trapped, but he heads in the opposite direction, toward the kitchen. New Guy follows behind him, his gaze roaming over the suits of armor standing at attention, the blue and red shields hanging from the fake stone walls.

"It happened during a tournament. I was thrown from my horse, you see," Alan says, squinting hard, like he's actually remembering something that happened to him and not to, you know, someone else entirely. " 'Tis the reason I am now forced to use this." He waves his cane in the air, just missing Julia as she tries to sneak behind him. Before she can get away, I drop into a full curtsey. A few of the little potatoes bounce off the platters and onto the stone floor. "Her Grace cometh," I say.

Julia scowls at me. Now that Alan knows she's there, she has no choice but to come over. Alan has even been known to send his queen to the stocks on occasion.

I give her an apologetic shrug before speed walking to table nine. Things have gone downhill since my last appearance ten minutes ago. The table is a mess, covered in broken crayons and the shredded pieces of a cardboard crown. The mother is mediating an argument between her two young sons over the remaining crown, while the father taps away on his phone.

"Here we go," I say, waiting for someone to clear a space on the table so I can set down their dinner. After it becomes apparent no one is going to help me, I give up and plop the platters on top of the mess.

The trays are barely out of my hands before the boys are grasping at the food like little savages. There are two turkey legs, one for each of them—their parents didn't order dinner; I guess greasy medieval food doesn't appeal to everyone—but the boys fight over the leg that is slightly bigger. Boy Number

One manages to grab hold of it first, which results in Boy Number Two knocking him over the head with one of the foam swords sold in our gift shop. In the ensuing frenzy, a goblet—also sold in our gift shop—is sent flying. It's full of milk. Every drop of which lands on me.

Awesome.

The mother sighs—*what can you do?*—while the cold liquid seeps through the bodice of my velvet costume, right through to my skin.

"'Tis no problem," I say. Wasted breath, as no one seems to be worried that I'm now stuck in a wet costume for the rest of my shift.

I trudge back to the kitchen. Amy is scraping food scraps off a plate into a big green garbage bin by the dishwashing station. It's steamy and smelly back here, like old fried food.

"Table nine?" she asks, catching sight of me. She sets the plate on top of a towering stack of dirty dishes waiting to be loaded into the industrial dishwasher.

I nod, feeling miserable.

Amy passes me a rag. "Cheer up. Only three hours till closing."

I dab at the stain but it's no use. The velvet has soaked up the milk and rubbing at it only seems to make it worse. Also, the fluff from the white rag is now sticking to the dark material.

Most nights aren't this bad. Most nights I actually like

working here. And not only because I need the money, although I do. I'm saving for the school band trip to London in the fall.

I've wanted to go to England since I was a kid and my gran would tell me stories about growing up in London after the war. She used to go back every year and she'd always bring the best stuff home for me—magnets shaped like Big Ben, a snow globe of Buckingham Palace. All kinds of British chocolate.

I can hardly believe I'll be there in a matter of months.

I'm still rubbing fruitlessly at the stain when Joe sidles up beside me. He's dressed in a green brocade long vest, black breeches, and shiny, knee-high black boots.

"Quinn. Excellent. I've been looking for you," he says, clapping a hand on my shoulder. "I'd like you to meet the newest addition to the Tudor Tymes team."

New Guy is beside him. He's a few inches taller than me, with wide shoulders that strain against his billowy pirate shirt. The eye not covered by the patch is a stormy gray. When he pushes the pirate hat back on his head and out of his face, I catch a glimpse of shaggy blond hair.

Definitely cute.

I smile at him, ready to welcome him to our strange little world, when he lifts the eye patch and I fully see his face.

"No need for introductions," New Guy says with a smirk. "Q and I go way back."

The smile freezes on my face. Because even though it's been five years and he's now taller than me and has a light scruff of facial hair, I recognize that smirk. Of course I do.

Wesley James.

Oh fie.

two.

"You two know each other?" Joe's eyebrows lift in surprise. "Huh. Small world."

Yes. Too small. Way, way too small.

I glance warily at Wesley. "I thought you moved to Portland."

He snaps the eye patch back over his eye. "And San Francisco. And Chicago. And Vegas," he says. "But my mom has always wanted to move back to Seattle, so . . . here we are. Again."

Here you are again, indeed.

I stuff the rag into my apron and glance at Joe. "I have a table waiting. I should probably get back out there."

"Do me a favor and take Wesley with you," Joe says. "Show him the ropes."

Ugh, really? It's a struggle to keep the smile on my face, but I can't exactly refuse my boss. Not without explaining why. I don't want anyone to know my history with Wesley James, so I turn on my heel and lead him through the kitchen to the small bar tucked in the back. *Bar* may be a bit of a misnomer, since we don't actually serve alcohol. What we have is a soda fountain, an espresso machine, and a few gallons of milk tucked into a small glass-front refrigerator.

"So, Q. It's been, what? Four years?" Wesley watches as I grab a carton of milk and start to fill a plastic goblet stamped with the Tudor Tymes logo—a silver crest with a monogram of two interlocking *T*s.

I can feel him assessing me, marking the changes since we last saw each other. My hair is longer, but still blond and curlier than I'd like it to be. I also have a lot more happening in the chestal area than I used to, which, judging from the way Wesley's staring, he's definitely noticed. It makes me wish I had a sweater or jacket or something to cover up with.

I may look physically different, but I still feel the same inside.

I still Hate. His. Guts.

"Five, actually," I say, sticking the milk carton back into the fridge. I set the goblet on a round silver tray along with a wicker basket lined with blue cloth.

"So fill me in. What have you been up to?"

What have I been up to? Hm. How to boil it down? Well, my parents got a divorce and my dad has pretty much been living like a nomad, bouncing from job to job. Still struggling with his gambling addiction, thanks for asking. Oh, and my gran, well, we had to put her in a home a couple of months ago. She has Alzheimer's.

And all of this is your fault, Wesley James. Well, maybe not the part about Gran getting Alzheimer's; I guess I can't blame him for that. But he's definitely had a hand in everything else.

This isn't exactly the place to unload on him, though, so I just say, "Stuff."

"Stuff?" Wesley shakes his head. "Yeah, that really doesn't tell me anything."

Kind of the point.

I use a pair of tongs to pinch two rolls from underneath the heat lamp. There's a beat of silence while Wesley waits for me to hold up my end of the conversation. This is the part where I'm supposed to ask him what his life has been like, how he's spent the past five years. When I don't, he jumps back in, like I knew he would. Wesley never could stand silence.

"Well, I see one thing hasn't changed," he says. "You haven't outgrown your fascination with all things English." He catches the surprise on my face. "It's why you're working here, right?"

I nod, dropping the rolls into the basket. "I can't believe you remember that."

"I remember a lot of things about you," he says.

I remember things about you, too. And none of them are good.

Wesley reaches past me, grabs the rolls out of the basket, and starts to juggle them. Which is not only weird but completely unhygienic. "How's your gran?"

The mention of Gran makes my heart squeeze. I guess that must show on my face, too, because Wesley stops mid-juggle. "Wait . . . she's not . . . ?"

I shake my head. "Still alive." *If you can call it that.*

His face relaxes in relief. "Great. You know, I'd love to see her. Catch up."

Not going to happen. Wesley's already taken so much from me. I'm not letting him have Gran, too.

"You know, juggling with the food is generally frowned upon," I say.

"Whoops. Sorry. Force of habit," he says sheepishly, dropping the rolls back in the basket.

I toss the soiled buns in the garbage and grab some fresh ones. Lifting up the tray, I push through the kitchen door and make my way, once again, to table nine. Fortunately, it's a slow night and I only have the one table to worry about.

The kids seem to have settled down, probably because they're stuffed full of nutritious, deep-fried turkey. I set the milk down in front of Boy Number One and place the basket in the center of the table. They didn't ask for more bread, but sometimes more bread is the key to getting a better tip. Or any kind of tip.

"How now." I bob a curtsey. "Prithee, I'd like to introduce—"

"Captain Grimbeard," Wesley interjects, extending his hand to give each boy a hearty handshake. They stare at him, awestruck. Clearly, pirate trumps royal servant in the eyes of eight-year-old boys.

"Um, yeah. Anyway," I say. "Captain Grimbread—"

"Grim*beard*."

"Captain Grimbeard is assisting me tonight. Pray tell, can I get thee anything else?"

It's like I haven't even spoken, these kids are so into Wesley and his stupid eye patch.

"You lads like magic?" Wesley reaches over and pulls a Tudor Tymes chocolate coin from behind Boy Number Two's ear, a totally lame trick that somehow manages to delight the entire table. They erupt in applause like he's David Copperfield or something.

A few minutes later, I'm pushed aside while Wesley makes balloon animals—which, *hello*, they totally did not have balloons in the Middle Ages. And even if they did, they were probably sheep bladders or something, and they almost certainly didn't use them to make balloon animals.

When the trumpet sounds to signal the start of the show, I

shepherd Wesley to the back of the room, where the waitstaff are supposed to remain, hidden in the shadows. I guess this is to make sure that none of us distract the audience from the real show—i.e., Alan.

"So, you're, like, a pirate magician?" I whisper to Wesley as the lights dim.

He smiles. "Cool, huh?"

"That doesn't even make sense," I say. "Pirates don't do magic tricks. They rape and pillage."

"You're thinking of Vikings."

Clearly, I need to bone up on my pirate history.

"Okay, fine. But I know for a fact that they didn't have magicians in the Middle Ages."

"Well . . . technically, the king had fools—"

I can't help but smile.

"—but you're right—they were more like clowns than magicians," he says. "But who doesn't love magic?" ·

Right now? I'm not so fond of it. Unless, of course, Wesley's able to make himself disappear. That I could definitely get behind.

"I can't believe you're still so into it," I say. Wesley used to carry a magic wand with him everywhere. But that was when we were eleven.

He shrugs. "Some things stick with you."

I can't argue with that. After all, as he pointed out earlier,

I've been borderline obsessed with England for years. That probably seems just as weird to him.

"Explain the balloon animals, then," I say. "Not something magicians normally do."

"I worked the birthday party circuit in Vegas."

"Wow. That's . . ."

"Geeky?" Wesley smiles. "Go on. You can say it. But I'll be laughing all the way to the bank." He holds up a five-dollar bill and nods toward table nine.

I narrow my eyes and make a grab for the bill, but he holds it out of my reach. "That's my tip, you ass! I earned it."

He folds the money into his pants pocket, where he knows I'm not about to go after it. "Maybe we can work out an arrangement. Magicians always need assistants."

Is he kidding? He started working here *an hour ago*. As if I'm going to help him with his stupid tricks!

I cross my arms, fuming, as Alan waddles onto the stage and settles himself on the throne. He clears his throat and begins to deliver a somber Shakespearean soliloquy. Because this is Alan's idea of a show small children are dying to see.

"I come no more to make you laugh," he booms, tapping his gold-tipped cane against the stage floor. "Things now, that bear a weighty and a serious brow . . . sad, high, and working . . . full of state and woe . . . such noble scenes as draw the eye to flow."

Alan loves a dramatic pause, so it usually takes him forever to wander through this soliloquy. Surprisingly, no one ever leaves during his performance. Maybe they're afraid he'll throw them in the stocks.

"You go to West Seattle High?" Wesley asks.

"Yup." I glance at him, my stomach suddenly tight. "Don't tell me . . ."

He nods. "I'll be there in the fall."

Great. So not only do I have to work with Wesley, but he'll be haunting my school hallways as well. This night just keeps getting better.

"It seriously sucks to have to start a new school in my senior year," he says. "I kept in touch with a couple of guys from elementary school, though, so at least I'm not going in totally blind." He nudges me with his elbow. "And you, of course. I know you."

Is he for real?

Wesley James and I will never be friends.

Ever.

He takes in my crossed arms, the death-glare. And, finally, he gets it.

"Wait," he says, his smile fading. "You aren't still mad . . ."

When I don't say anything, Wesley shakes his head. "Boy, Q. You can really hold a grudge."

He has no idea.

"How can you still be mad? It was *five years ago*," he says. "And, when you think about it, I didn't even really do anything—"

"I don't want to talk about it," I snap. The words come out louder than I expected them to, falling right into one of Alan's dramatic pauses. I sink back into the shadows before he can identify me—I'm hoping the stage lights mean he can't see the crowd clearly—and I don't breathe again until he resumes his speech.

As soon as the lights come up, I leave Wesley to fend for himself.

By the time I get home, it's nearly midnight. I text Erin—fortunately, she's a night owl—and a few seconds later my phone rings.

"I hate my life," I say, collapsing on my bed. I really should take a shower—I stink like turkey and grease and despair—but right now I need to talk to Erin more than I need to be clean. "You will not believe who I'm working with."

"Who?"

"I can't say his name. I'm too traumatized." I throw my arm over my eyes.

"Jason Cutler?"

Jason and I had a brief thing last semester. He dumped me

over text the day before my birthday, so I understand why his name is the first to pop into her head.

But while working with Jason would be heinous, it would still be preferable to working with Wesley.

"Worse," I say.

"Who's worse than Jason?"

"Wesley James."

"No! I thought he lived in Oregon?"

I sigh deeply and turn over, burying my face in my pillow. "He moved back," I mumble.

"What are you going to do?"

I picture Erin in her room. It's twice the size of mine, with purple-striped walls and a canopy bed, like something out of a fairy tale.

"What can I do?" I say.

"I don't know. Quit?"

"Not if I want to go to London. It's way too late in the summer to try to find another job. Besides, why should I quit? I was there first."

"Maybe it won't be so bad," she says. "Maybe he's changed."

"No. He hasn't." I rub my eyes. I think I'm getting a migraine.

"Is he cute?"

"Erin."

"What? He was a cute kid. I'm trying to get a mental picture of what he looks like now."

"You don't need a mental picture. You can see him in person when he starts school with us in September."

"Seriously?"

"Why do you sound excited? This is the exact opposite of exciting news."

She laughs. "I don't know. Maybe because all you've talked about for years is what a jerk he is. How he ruined your life. I just think . . ."

"You just think what?" I prompt.

"Sixth grade was a long time ago, Quinn. People change," she says. "Maybe it's time to let go."

Erin doesn't get it. Wesley and his big mouth are the reason my parents are no longer together. That's not something I will let go of. Ever.

In the background, I can hear her fingers clicking the keys on her saxophone. "You're practicing?"

"I'm not actually playing. My mom would kill me if I woke her up. I'm working on my finger technique."

Erin's very serious about music. I glance guiltily at my clarinet case leaning against the wall in the corner of my room. I haven't pulled it out since band practice last week. Mr. Aioki is forcing us to meet over the summer so we'll be ready for the tour, but we're also supposed to practice on our own, too. And I never seem to get around to it.

"So, how much did you make tonight?" Erin asks.

I dig in my pocket and pull out a few wrinkled bills and some coins, along with the stinky milk rag I forgot to dump in the restaurant's laundry bin. "Thirteen bucks." At this rate, I should get to London around my fortieth birthday.

I sit up and grab for the mason jar on my bedside table. It's nearly full, which makes me feel a tiny bit better. I know without counting that there's almost three hundred dollars inside. I like to wait until it's completely full before depositing the money into my account.

"Every little bit, right?" Erin says.

I stuff the money into the jar and the coins make a satisfying clink against the glass. "Every little bit."

three.

I find Caleb restocking the science fiction section. He's crouched down, sliding a stack of paperbacks onto the wide wooden shelves.

"Hey." I nudge him with my flip-flop, and my clarinet case bumps against my leg.

"Hey." Caleb straightens the books so the spines are all perfectly lined up and then stands. He's wearing a green polo shirt and khakis with knife-blade creases running down each leg. It's not even a uniform; this is just the way Caleb dresses. Like a middle-aged man.

"You're early." He checks his watch. "Practice isn't for another half an hour."

Caleb is the other clarinet player in concert band. He's

better than me—by a mile—but that's because he actually cares about playing the clarinet.

"I know. I thought I'd check out the travel section," I say.

He smiles. "Again?"

"I think I'll actually pull the trigger this time." I've been eyeing an art book on England. I haven't bought it though because it's superexpensive and I'm trying to pinch every penny I can. But I've decided I need something to cheer me up after last night.

"You can use my employee discount," he offers. "Twenty-five percent."

"Thanks."

Caleb tells me he'll meet me at the register and I wander to the other side of the store, where the travel books are kept. It's a small section tucked near the in-store café, so the whole area smells like roasting coffee and banana bread.

I set my case on the floor, grab *England's Greatest Attractions* from the shelf, and flop into a squashy yellow chair. Once I'm settled, I open the book to page 67, the place I always start. Big Ben. Looking at the photo makes my heart beat a little bit faster. My grandfather proposed to my gran on Westminster Bridge, at the foot of that famous old clock, more than fifty years ago. It's the first place I want to go when I finally get to London.

I'm so busy going over the long list of things I need to see and how I'm going to accomplish all of them in the small amount of free time Mr. Aioki is allotting us, that I don't notice the black Converse sneakers at first. When I look up, it's straight into a pair of dark gray eyes.

Wesley James is standing in front of me in a rumpled T-shirt, his blond hair all mussed like he's just come in from a windstorm. The sight of him unexpectedly sends a nervous jolt through me.

"Well, looky here," he says. He's holding a large takeout coffee cup.

"You're not supposed to bring food or drinks into this part of the store," I say.

The corner of Wesley's mouth lifts up, a half smile. For some reason I can't figure out, he seems to find me amusing. "Q, you are way too uptight. What are they going to do? Kick me out?" He takes a sip of his coffee, like he's daring me to tell on him.

And you know what? I'm considering it.

"What are you doing here anyway?" I don't like that he's hovering over me—it's like it gives him the upper hand, somehow—so I struggle out of the squashy chair. "Are you following me? Because I'm pretty sure stalking is a federal offense."

"I'm not stalking you, crazy," he says. "I'm here to see a friend. I happened to be over there"—he points at the café— "when I saw you over here. Thought I'd say hi."

Oh.

"Okay, well. Hi." I lean down to pick up my clarinet case. Wesley takes advantage of the fact that I've relaxed my guard and plucks the book from my hand.

"*England's Greatest Attractions.*" He glances at me. I can't read the expression on his face, but I immediately feel defensive.

"It's research," I say. "I'm going to London. With the school band."

I have no idea why I'm telling him this. The less Wesley knows about me and my life, the better. He can't be trusted. He proved that a long time ago.

"Really?" He sets his coffee on the narrow arm of the chair, where it will almost definitely tip and spill all over the pale leather, and flips the book open. He paws recklessly through the pages, flipping past photos of Buckingham Palace and Stonehenge. "Hm. Maybe I should join band. I'd love to go to England."

"Sorry." I snatch the book back, almost catching his fingers as I snap the cover closed. "Not possible. It's concert band. You have to audition to get in."

"Shouldn't be a problem," he says. "I play the tuba."

"You're kidding, right?" 'Cause it must be a joke. The Wesley I knew was way too cool to go near a tuba. He was more of a guitar or drums kind of guy.

He cocks his head. And there's that half smile again. "Nope."

I snort.

"Oh, you think that's funny? Okay. So what do you play?"

Crap. I really should think before I snort.

"The clarinet," I mumble.

Wesley makes a big deal of holding his hand up to his ear. "I'm sorry, what? I didn't hear you."

"The clarinet," I snap. "I play the clarinet. Which, as everyone knows, is much cooler than the tuba." I march away but he trails after me. He follows me all the way to the front register, where Caleb is waiting.

I set the book on the counter. Wesley's right beside me, all up in my personal space, so I turn around and hiss, "Why are you still here?"

"I told you. I'm here to see a friend." He extends his hand to Caleb and they do some weirdly complicated boy handshake that makes my heart sink.

Wesley did mention he'd kept in touch with some of the guys from elementary school.

"So what's up, man? Did you get the job?" Caleb asks as he rings up my book.

I hand him my debit card, trying to keep my expression calm. Inside, though, I'm a tornado. Because I know what's coming. I know exactly what Wesley will say next. And I can't think of a way to stop him.

"Yup. In fact Q and I work together," he says.

And there it is. Another secret spilled by Wesley James.

Caleb's eyebrows fly up into his hairline. "You work at Tudor Tymes, Quinn? You never mentioned that."

It's not exactly something I go around broadcasting. Most of my friends don't even know, with the exception of Erin. I was teased in middle school, so I've learned not to give anyone any ammunition. Working in a medieval restaurant is just asking for it.

"I loved that place when I was a kid," Caleb says. "Which character are you?"

Wesley chuckles. "She's a wench."

"I am *not* a wench," I say, glaring at him. "I'm a royal servant."

"Please." Wesley drains his coffee. He shoots the empty cup over the counter and it sinks perfectly into the small metal garbage can behind Caleb. "She's definitely a wench. She wears a corset."

They both stare at me, like they're picturing me in it right now, which is totally humiliating. I cross my arms over my chest to block their view. "Yeah, well, he's a pirate magician." I make a face like, *isn't-that-the-stupidest-thing-you've-ever-heard*, but Caleb doesn't catch it. He's busy shoving my book into a recycled tote bag.

"You're still doing magic, dude?" he says.

"Helps with the tips," Wesley mutters.

"You mean it helps you steal tips." I take the bag from Caleb. "We should probably get going. I don't want to be late for practice."

"Yeah." Caleb takes off his name tag and slides it into his pocket. "You ready?" he says to Wesley.

Wait, what?

"Wes is coming with us. He's thinking about buying my truck, so I told him to come for a test drive. You don't mind, do you?"

Mind? Of course I mind. But I don't know how I can tell Caleb that without seeming like a total freak.

And so that is how I end up wedged between them, Caleb on one side and Wesley on the other. I'm scrunched over on the bench seat as close to Caleb as possible, but Wesley's knee still somehow keeps brushing against mine.

"How come you're selling your truck?" I ask Caleb.

He grimaces. "The payments are killing me. And with London coming up . . ." He doesn't need to finish the sentence. Europe is not cheap. Sure, the band is holding fund-raisers to offset some of the cost, but each of us is still expected to kick in almost fifteen hundred dollars. Not all of our parents can afford it. Some of us have to sell our trucks or get jobs in medieval-themed restaurants.

We drive down California Avenue, past boutiques and

coffee shops, bakeries and thrift stores, past a whole lifetime of memories. I let Wesley and Caleb carry the conversation—mostly about horsepower and gas mileage, eventually segueing into a debate about the Seattle Seahawks that I don't even try to follow, until we reach West Seattle High. Caleb and I climb out and Caleb tells Wesley to pick us up after practice. So I guess I haven't seen the last of him today.

Our footsteps echo in the halls. It's so weird to be here in the summer, when the school is deserted. The walls are freshly painted, no flyers or posters to clutter them up. It even smells different. Cleaner.

We slip into the band room. Erin's at the back with the other saxophones. She smiles until she notices I'm with Caleb then she shakes her head. She doesn't think I should hang out with him so much, considering he likes me and I haven't made up my mind about him yet.

On paper, Caleb is perfect for me. There are a million reasons why I should like him. He's smart and responsible. He's not bad to look at. He plays the clarinet. We're a match made in band geek heaven.

But.

He does not make my knees weak. Or my heart race or give me butterflies or any of those other clichéd feelings you're supposed to have when you like someone. But I'm hoping that will change.

I'm almost finished assembling my clarinet when Mr. Aioki pulls the door closed and steps up to the podium. He taps his baton against the metal and lifts his arms. As the rest of the band members raise their instruments, I quickly place my reed against the mouthpiece and slide the ligature over the top to keep the reed in place, trying to ignore the annoyed expression on my band teacher's face.

The sound of Beethoven's March in D Major floods the room, pushing Wesley and everything else out of my mind.

four.

Dad's already in line when I arrive at the crumpet place. We've been meeting here for breakfast every Saturday morning since the divorce.

"Hey, ladybug," he says, giving me a hug. He smells like aftershave. A good sign. He must have won at the track last night. When he loses—which happens often—he reeks like beer. "There's a free table over there."

I hurry over and snag the table that overlooks the guy making the crumpets. While Dad places our order, I watch the guy behind the window squeeze thick yellow batter into the tiny, round metal pans and then place them on the griddle.

"So," Dad says, setting a blackberry-jam-covered crumpet in front of me and sliding into his chair. "How's your mother?"

"Good." It's the same answer I give him every time he asks, which is every time I see him. He still seems to think he has a chance of winning her back. I don't have the heart to tell him it's never going to happen.

Dad dumps a packet of sugar into his mug and then stirs his coffee, his spoon clinking against the porcelain. "And how's the job going?"

I shrug. I should probably tell him that the Jameses are back in town, but he's between jobs again and it might make him feel bad. No need to remind him about the past. It's bad enough I have to deal with it.

"I'm going to London in the fall with band," I say. This is the first time I've mentioned the trip, even though I've known about it since last semester. There hasn't been much point in talking about it with him until I was sure I'd have enough money to go.

"Really? That sounds fun." His voice wavers. He's already worrying about how he's going to pay for it.

"I should have the full amount saved by the time school starts," I say.

His face relaxes. "I didn't realize you guys were so good."

"Eh. We're okay. It's not a competition or anything. It's just a tour."

Dad leans back in his chair, a faraway look in his eyes. "Did I ever tell you about the time I went to Amsterdam with—"

"—your high school choir. Your club came in fourth but it was still the best life experience ever."

He smiles. "Well, maybe not ever. But close," he says.

Dad rhapsodizes about his long-ago boyhood adventures in the Netherlands for the rest of breakfast. There's something sad about his memories, maybe because that high school trip was the one and only time he's ever left Washington State. And probably the only time he ever will.

When he gets up to go to the bathroom, I dig four dollars out of my wallet and tuck it underneath the plates. Dad isn't a big tipper and ever since I started working at a restaurant, I'm hyperaware of tipping well.

I'm waiting at the door when he returns. It looks like it's going to rain and I'm debating whether I should ask him to drive me to Gran's. As far as I know, he hasn't been back to the house since Aunt Celia kicked him out last month, but maybe it's time he went. He can't avoid the situation—or his sister—forever.

"Um . . . do you think you could drop me off at Gran's? I told Celia I'd help her get the house ready."

She's putting it on the market next week. He really should be the one helping her clean it out, not me, but I can tell from the pinched look on his face when I mention her name that that isn't going to happen. My dad and his sister have never seen eye to eye and Gran's illness has only made things worse.

"Sure," he says.

I follow him across the street to his busted-looking Honda. He still hasn't gotten the muffler fixed and it's almost dragging on the ground. When I climb into the passenger seat, I notice he's used duct tape to repair a rip in the leather seat.

"What's Celia planning to do with everything?" Dad asks, starting the car. He took all of the furniture from his bedroom when he left last month, but there's probably a lot of other stuff that he could use. Or that he might want for sentimental reasons. I also know that there's no way Celia will let him have anything. She already thinks he's taken too much.

"I think she's storing some of it." And selling the rest. The place Gran's in is expensive and Celia doesn't hide the fact that the extra money is necessary for Gran's care.

Dad's fingers tighten on the steering wheel. I know he's worried his sister will cut him out completely, but even I have to admit it's better for her to hold the reins when it comes to Gran's finances. My dad means well—he always means well—but his gambling problem makes it hard to trust him sometimes. Especially with money.

The small moving van Celia rented is blocking the driveway. I wasn't really holding out much hope that Dad would come in and help us, so I'm not surprised when he doesn't shut off the car when he pulls over to the curb.

This is the house he grew up in and I know he doesn't

agree with selling it, but there doesn't seem to be another choice. Not according to Celia anyway. She lives a very together life in San Francisco with her partner, Kathy, and their four rescue dogs, and Dad certainly can't afford to buy the place. There really is no other option.

"Just make sure she doesn't get rid of everything, okay?" he says.

I nod, even though I'm not sure what, in all of Gran's stuff, he'd like to keep. What exactly he thinks is worth saving.

"What about this?" I hold up a chipped porcelain cherub. It's actually pretty creepy, a disembodied head with wings growing out of it. I have no idea why Gran has this. Why she has half this stuff.

Celia glances up from a file box marked TAX RETURNS. She wrinkles her nose and points to the growing mountain of junk in the corner. So far, pretty much everything I've shown her has landed in the junk pile.

Not that I blame her. I don't want most of this stuff, either. But still, it feels weird, dividing up Gran's things like this. I mean, she's still alive.

She couldn't take much with her to the home—just a few personal effects. Celia plans to store all Gran's furniture, including the old, creaky brass bed I'm sitting on, until we figure out what to do with it. I think she's hoping I'll take the bed one day when I move out on my own.

I gently toss the cherub on top of an ugly, pilled green afghan then remove the lid off the shoe box I found wedged underneath Gran's bed. The box is stuffed full of awkward-stage photos of my dad and Celia, in bell-bottoms and turtle-necks. I pull out one of Dad with a Fu Manchu mustache. Or what would be a Fu Manchu if he had more than a few strands of facial hair.

I snicker. "Now this I'm keeping." I flip the photo over so Celia can see it.

She smiles and shakes her head. "He thought a mustache would make him look older. Help him get girls."

Her smile fades. I know it's hard for her to understand how my dad ended up broke, jobless, and living with his mother. But I know exactly how he ended up there. And it's not his fault. Not completely anyway.

I stick the photo back in the shoe box and place the box with the other things I'm keeping. All things that most remind me of my gran: her faded double wedding ring quilt, her silver watch. A delicate blue teacup.

After a while, Celia stands up and pushes her knuckles into her back to work out the kinks. She runs the tip of her finger over the top of Gran's dresser. "I didn't know things were this bad," she says, showing me her dust-coated finger. "Your gran always kept this place spotless. You could have eaten off the floors."

I know Celia doesn't blame me for not telling her that Gran was getting worse, but I still feel sick with guilt. I can't bring myself to tell her that I didn't know. The truth is, I haven't seen Gran much over the past year. Not enough to notice things were this bad.

I get off the bed and open her closet. Gran always dressed up—she's never owned a pair of jeans—and her closet is full of Easter-colored suits and dresses. Patent leather shoes, handbags. Scarves. Not the elastic-waist pants and shoes with rubber soles she's trapped in now. The sight of her fancy clothes overwhelms me. I want to burrow into her closet and close the door. Maybe never come out.

"Why don't we take a break?" Celia says, brushing her dusty hands on her jeans. My chest feels tight as I follow her down the hallway and into the kitchen.

I spent a lot of time in this house as a kid. Entire days during the summer, since my parents both worked. Gran and I would bake gingersnaps and watch the Hallmark movies she'd taped on her ancient VCR. But the best times were when she'd tell me stories about growing up in London. Where she went to school, how she met my grandfather.

The last full summer I spent with her was when I was

eleven. And it was no longer just the two of us. Gran was watching Wesley, too.

Celia takes two cans of ginger ale out of the fridge. She hands one of them to me and we sit at the glass-topped kitchen table, the one bound for the Salvation Army.

"Have you ever been to England?" I ask her.

She nods. "Once. Right after college."

"I'm going in the fall. With concert band."

"I didn't know you were in concert band," she says. "What do you play?"

"The clarinet."

She makes a face. "Really?"

"It's better than the tuba," I say.

"So when are you going?"

"November." I roll the can of soda between my palms. "I was wondering . . . do you know where the house Gran grew up in is? I'd like to see where she lived."

Celia reaches over and squeezes my hand. "I think I have the address somewhere."

I know that visiting all of the places Gran's told me about won't make a difference. It won't miraculously help her remember me. But I'm hoping that, if I'm really lucky, maybe it just might help me remember her.

five.

I slip behind the front desk, nudging Rachel aside so I can check out my assigned section. Rachel's on the phone, taking a reservation. Her hair is gathered in a fake braided brown bun. Her actual hair is short but since girls in medieval times did not do short hair, management insists she wear this heinous clip-on.

"For tonight?" Rachel chews her bottom lip. "Okay, yes. We can fit you in. No problem." She scribbles "party of sixteen" on the glass map of the restaurant, over the icon of the long oak table we use for large parties.

My heart begins to pound. The only parties we get at Tudor Tymes are kids' birthday parties. And kids' birthday parties are the worst. THE WORST. Food always ends up everywhere.

The last time I worked one, it took me forty-five minutes to grout out all the mashed food embedded in the cracks in the stone floor.

Rachel must sense my panic because she points the tip of her pen at my name, scrawled over tables ten through seventeen. My section.

I sag with relief. It doesn't mean I'm totally off the hook. I still have to sing. Yes, we are one of those annoying restaurants that sing to you on your birthday. And force you to wear a huge purple-and-yellow jester's hat.

Rachel writes Wesley's name above the birthday party— ha!—then adds Amy as well. Wesley hasn't been here long enough to work a party on his own, so she's stuck helping him. Poor Amy. She hates working birthday parties more than I do.

I squeeze past Rachel and head down the hall, past the gift shop, through the kitchen, and into the staff room.

Wesley's on the couch. He's wearing his ridiculous pirate costume, his black-booted feet propped up on the coffee table, spinning a magic wand in his fingers.

"Hey," he says, dropping his feet to the floor. His heavy boots clunk against the linoleum.

Ignoring him, I yank open one of the small lockers lining the wall and stuff my messenger bag inside. Slamming the metal door shut, I pull the tiny key from the lock. I keep my back to him as I fasten the safety pin dangling off the key to the inside of my corset. Don't want to accidentally treat him to a peep show.

The gong rings, signaling that the drawbridge is about to be lowered. All staff—with the exception of their Royal Highnesses, King Henry and Queen Catherine—are supposed to be up front to welcome guests when the doors open. Restaurant policy.

I hurry down the hall, tying my apron on behind my back, and arrive at the doors as the last gong sounds. As Joe unbolts the huge, curved wooden door, Wesley steps in line. I peer around him at Bruce and Rachel, standing at attention.

There's no sign of Amy.

Wait. Where is Amy?

The door starts to creak open, spilling sunlight onto the floor. I try to catch Rachel's eye, but she's avoiding looking at me. Which can only mean . . .

"Sorry, Quinn." She hands me a thick stack of paper crowns. "Amy called in sick."

This is not good. I can't be stuck working with Wesley tonight. Or any night.

I shoot a pleading glance at Bruce.

"No way," he says. "I'm still recovering from yesterday. Twenty-three six-year-olds." He shudders.

"Okay, well. Wesley, I'm sure you can handle it." I shove the paper crowns at him.

"Quinn, he's never worked a party before," Rachel says. "He doesn't know what he's doing."

"I really don't." Wesley smiles.

This sucks. And there is no way to make it un-suck, either, unless Amy shows up. The chance of that being zero. There's no longer any time to worry about it, though, because customers have started to trickle in.

"Good eventide, my lord, my lady." I curtsey to an older couple hustling in two small girls dressed as princesses. "Thou art very pretty." The girls stare at me, eyes wide.

As they pass by Wesley, he waves a foam sword at them. "Arrrrrgh," he says in pirate-brogue. The little girls screech and hide behind their mother's pencil skirt.

"Nice work," I say.

"Yeah, that kind of played out differently in my mind," he says as their mother ushers them away.

Once the first wave of customers has entered, Wesley and I head to our table to get ready for the party. I point to the paper crowns he's almost crumpling in his hand. "Put one at each place setting."

"I don't remember you being so bossy," he mumbles. He starts to place them around the table haphazardly. When I follow behind, straightening them, Wesley stops and glares at me. "Okay that? Is very annoying."

"Actually, what's annoying is having to fix them," I say. "If you put them down right in the first place—"

He shakes his head. "Q, you seriously need to relax."

You know what doesn't relax me? Being told to relax.

"I can't do this," I say. "You're on your own. I'm going to talk to Joe."

I'll beg him to make Bruce work the party with Wesley. Sure, Bruce will probably hate my guts, but it's totally worth it if it means I'm not stuck with Wesley all night.

"And say what? That you don't want to play with me?" He smirks. "You'll have to tell him why. And what are you going to say?" In a high falsetto voice that doesn't sound anything like mine, he says, "Well, Joe, it's all because back in sixth grade Wesley told—"

"Okay," I cut him off. "Fine." I straighten the last paper crown. "Why do you want to work with me anyway?"

Wesley sighs. "Because, Q, believe it or not, I want to be friends."

Friends. That is never going to happen.

"And I can see I have my work cut out for me," he says. "Has anyone ever told you that you're really stubborn?"

Yes. But whatever.

We finish the table and the kids arrive. Once they are settled into their seats, I fill their water goblets and take their orders, while Wesley jacks around, entertaining everyone with card tricks. It's beyond annoying. And it's definitely not the path to earning my friendship. By the time the mom signals that they're ready for cake, I've done most of the work and I'm officially pissed off.

I drag Wesley away from the applause and into the kitchen. The birthday boy's parents brought a huge sheet cake topped with a plastic pirate ship. The cake weighs about seven hundred pounds, so I order Wesley to grab it from the cooler. He rolls his eyes, but I guess he can tell from the look on my face that he shouldn't mess with me, because he does it. When he comes back out of the cooler, I notice his finger is digging into the side of the cake.

"Seriously?"

He sets the cake on the counter, checks out the hole. "It's not that bad. I bet no one will even notice."

Not true. It is that bad. And someone will definitely notice.

I pick up a butter knife. Wesley takes a step away from me—as if I'd actually stab him in public!—and I smooth icing over the hole. It's not perfect but it'll have to do. And if the parents complain, I have no problem telling them that it's Wesley's fault.

On the way out of the kitchen, I toggle the light switch

near the door, making the lights flash, a signal to the rest of the staff that it's time to sing.

Wesley carries the cake out and sets it in front of the birthday boy. Bruce and Rachel wander over and we break into a rousing chorus of "Happy Birthday" while Rachel tunelessly strums the lute.

I forgot to bring plates so I send Wesley back to the kitchen to grab some. Turns out there is an upside to working this party with him after all—I get to tell him what to do. While he's gone, Alan arrives. A personal visit from the king is part of the premium birthday package.

"Well now. I hear 'tis young Sean's birthday," Alan says, patting the kid on the shoulder. "You know what we do to little boys on their birthdays?" He leans down so his wide, bearded face is only inches from the kid's. "We put them in the stocks!"

Sean starts to wail and the jester's hat bobs on his head, causing the tiny brass bells to ring. "I don't want to go!"

"Oh, come now, lad!" Alan booms. "It's great fun."

No, it's really not. I don't blame the kid for crying. I may have shed a tear or two the time I was stuck in there.

Just then, Wesley returns with the plates. And I get an idea. The best, most brilliant idea ever.

"It's okay, Sean." I pat the kid's bony shoulder. "You don't have to go. We'll send Captain Grimbutt instead."

Wesley's eyes narrow. "Grim*beard*. And send me where?"

Sean nods so enthusiastically, his hat falls off. All the kids stomp and cheer.

"Send me where?" Wesley repeats. I point to the huge wooden contraption in the corner, a single spotlight glinting evilly off the metal locks.

He swallows. "Uh . . . the thing is, I'm sort of claustrophobic . . ."

"Not to worry." I smile sweetly at him. "It doesn't actually lock. And we won't leave you in there long."

Just until the end of my shift.

Alan booms for Bruce, our "guard." He marches Wesley over to the stocks, unceremoniously shoves his head and hands through the holes, and snaps the gate closed. Wesley glares at me as best he can with his head bent at such a weird angle.

Feeling victorious—*how do you like working at Tudor Tymes now, Wesley James?*—I go back to serving the six-year-olds. I'm so busy keeping up with their demands that I forget about Wesley for a few minutes. Until I'm walking into the kitchen for more bread and I catch sight of him, hunched over and uncomfortable, his eyes squeezed shut. I guess he wasn't kidding when he said he's claustrophobic.

My elation at getting him thrown in the stocks starts to dissipate. Maybe this wasn't such a good idea. I want revenge, sure, but I don't want to kill him.

I walk over and bend down so Wesley can see my face. "Are you okay?"

"I'm fine," he says, but he doesn't open his eyes. His brow is scrunched up and sweaty, and all the color has left his cheeks.

I'm torn. As much as I want to help him—and, strangely, I do want to help him—I don't want to end up in the stocks myself. If Alan catches me trying to spring Wesley, I'm done for.

"It shouldn't be too much longer," I say.

He grunts.

I reach out to put my hand on his shoulder, but pull back before I make contact. *What am I doing?* Wesley James has been back in my life for five minutes and already I'm going soft. I should leave him here, let him do his time. It's no less than he deserves.

But he looks so miserable, I find myself heading to Joe's office to ask him to set Wesley free—Joe's the only one Alan will listen to. He's clearly annoyed that I'm bothering him, but when I tell him I can't work the birthday party all by myself, he sighs and comes with me.

"Thanks, Q," Wesley says after Joe springs him. I'm not sure whether he's thanking me for getting him sent to the stocks in the first place or for getting him out. There's no time to clarify—not that I really want to know anyway—because the birthday party has started to unravel. I spend five minutes coaxing a crying little girl from underneath the table while the rest of the kids clamor around Wesley, begging him for balloon animals.

An hour later, the kids are all gone and we're cleaning up. Or I'm cleaning up and Wesley's fooling around. I'm about to blast him for being lazy when he hands me a lumpy brown balloon with round orange eyes and two long white tusks.

I blink. "What is it?"

"It's a Gruffalo." He smiles and points to the sharp lines he's drawn near what I gather is the thing's mouth. "Those are his terrible teeth. And see, here are his terrible claws." He maneuvers the balloon monster in my hands so I can see the drawn-on claws. "You really can't tell?" He looks so crestfallen, I start to laugh.

For some reason, Wesley and I were obsessed with that book. Even though it was way too young for us, we made Gran read it over and over, the entire summer, because we liked the melody of her British accent.

I stop, mid-laugh, and straighten my face. He's obviously trying to jog a nice memory by giving this to me, remind me of a time when we used to be friends. I hate that it worked.

I toss the balloon on the table and finish clearing up. Wesley stands there for a second, confused, I think, by my sudden mood swing. I feel him watching me. I don't want him to see that he's reached me at all, so I busy myself with sweeping bread crumbs off the table until he finally gives up and wanders away.

An hour later, I'm waiting outside in the parking lot. Mom's supposed to pick me up, but she's not here, which is odd. I check my voice mail. She's working overtime at the hospital and I should call my dad to come and get me.

Great.

I know it's not her fault—my mom never passes up overtime. She can't afford to. But calling my dad? Pointless. He's probably at the track.

I'm debating whether I should try Erin when a white minivan pulls up to the curb. The passenger-side window rolls down and Wesley sticks his head out.

"Need a ride?" he asks.

I narrow my eyes. "So you can exact your revenge? No."

"Are you always this distrustful?"

"Yes."

He unlocks the door. "Come on, Q. Get in."

I could still try Erin, but it will take her at least half an hour to get here. I really just want to get home, so I sigh and climb inside. The floor mat is covered in Cheerios and little crackers shaped like fish. Two car seats are strapped to the bench seat in the back, a bursting diaper bag shoved between them.

"Whose van is this?"

"My parents'," he says. "They bought it after my sisters were born."

"You have sisters now?"

He nods. "Two. Twins, actually." He pulls into the street. "Ashby and Emily. They were sort of a surprise."

"For who? You or your parents?"

Wesley smiles. "Mostly for me. I knew my parents wanted more kids, but I didn't know how badly until my mom started fertility treatments."

I guess that explains why he wants to buy Caleb's truck. And why he's working at the restaurant. My mom used to work in a fertility clinic so I know the treatment is expensive. Add in the cost of raising two more kids . . . well, it probably means his mother doesn't just hand him money.

He glances at me. "I'm not complaining. It all worked out. My sisters are great."

I shouldn't ask him personal questions. I shouldn't be asking him *any* questions. I don't want to know about Wesley's life. I don't want him to give me any reason not to stay mad.

We drive for a few minutes in silence—through the university district and onto the freeway, over the bridge, the lights of downtown Seattle laid out before us. I can see the Space Needle in the distance. Safeco Field.

"So . . . your gran. Is she still in that big house on Queen Anne?" he asks.

"Nope." I don't elaborate. Just as I don't want to know anything about his life, I don't want him to know anything about mine.

But Wesley James doesn't give up easily.

"Like I said before, I'd love to visit her," he says. "Thank her for all the packages she sent us in Portland."

I stare at him. "What packages?"

Okay, I know I just made a pact with myself not to ask him any more questions, but this is different. I didn't know Gran kept in touch with the Jameses. Why would she keep in touch with them? Especially when she knew how I felt about Wesley. About what he did.

"She'd send me stuff, sometimes. Chocolate, comic books. That kind of thing," he says. "I guess she knew how upset I was about moving."

I can't help it. I feel totally betrayed. And the worst part is, I can't even ask Gran about this, because she won't remember. She doesn't remember anything anymore. Not even me.

Wesley turns the van onto my street. When we pass his old house, a blue Cape Cod six houses down from my own, he stops and rolls down the window.

"So who lives there now?" he asks.

"The Middlesteins." I slide open the passenger-side door and hop out. "Thanks for the ride."

"I can drive you the rest of the way, Q," he says.

But I pretend not to hear him. I just close the door and take off down the street.

six.

My dad's new apartment is in a supershady part of town. The kind of neighborhood where no one ventures outside after night falls, unless they are up to no good. I'm standing in front of his sad-looking building, holding the potted cactus I bought at a Korean market a few blocks away, wondering if surprising him is a good idea after all.

But I'm here. And I don't want to carry this cactus all the way to the crumpet place, where we're supposed to meet later, and I really do want to see his apartment. So I walk up the crumbling cement path to the front door.

Bloomfield Manor is spelled out in peeling gold cursive on the glass. A board with the tenants' names is mounted on the yellow-y white stucco wall beside the door. Dad is simply listed as "occupied." When I push the grimy button next to 218, nothing happens.

I take a step back, trying to decide what to do. I'm about to give up on the element of surprise and just call him when a lady with a Maltese puppy comes out. I catch the door before it swings shut. She dumps her dog on a small patch of brown grass, not at all bothered that she's just let a complete stranger into the building.

I take the stairs to the second floor. The hallway stinks of cooking oil and foreign spices. The carpets are almost worn through and the floor creaks like it's going to give out under my feet. And honestly? From what I've seen so far, I wouldn't be surprised if I fell right through to the lobby.

I can't believe my dad actually lives here. That *anyone* lives here.

I'm halfway down the hall when a man comes out of Dad's apartment. He's tall and burly, with curly black hair that touches his shoulders. He's wearing jeans and a white shirt, unbuttoned to show more chest hair than is ever necessary. I know he's bad news because my stomach lurches when our eyes meet.

He leers at me and when he passes by, I almost choke on his foul-smelling aftershave. When I reach Dad's door, I glance back at him. He's staring over his shoulder at me, too, and he gives me another sleazy little smile before thundering down the stairs.

Hands shaking, I knock. The door flies open immediately.

"I told you, I'll get the rest of it to you in a few—" Dad blinks at me, shocked. "Quinn," he says, sticking his head out and peering down the hall. "What are you doing here? I thought we were meeting at the restaurant."

"Uh, yeah. I thought . . . Well, I wanted to see your new place." I hand him the cactus. "Happy housewarming," I mutter.

Dad stares at the plant like he's never seen one before. Then he grabs my arm, yanks me inside, and locks the door.

First glance: bare white walls, a towering stack of newspapers, a bookshelf made of cinder blocks, a futon. It's like he's a struggling college student, one who can't even afford an IKEA bookshelf. The only bit of personality at all comes from the baseball autographed by Derek Jeter that my mom gave him for his birthday one year. His most prized possession.

I feel sick. His situation is even worse than I thought. And I didn't have high expectations to begin with.

"Who was that guy?" I try to keep my voice steady.

"Just an old friend," Dad says, smiling thinly. He swipes a hand across his forehead. "Is it hot in here?"

It's not, but he goes over to the window and pops it open anyway. He sets the cactus on one of Gran's old TV trays and then sinks down onto the futon. The thought of him sitting there alone, night after night, makes my heart hurt.

I sit down beside him. "Are you in some kind of trouble?"

"It's nothing you need to worry about, ladybug." He pats my knee, but I don't feel reassured. At all.

"Was he your bookie or something?"

"Quinn, honey, this really isn't something you need to concern yourself with."

I sigh. "How much do you owe him?"

He stands up, wipes his palms on his shorts. "We are not having this conversation. Please don't worry about it, okay? I'm handling it."

Right. Like he's handled it before.

I kind of want to kick him. Hard. Because he never learns. He's lost nearly everything—his job, his house, his family—but he still keeps gambling. I know it's an addiction, a sickness, but I have a hard time believing that he can't stop.

And now he's put himself in danger. That guy looked like he could easily break my dad's legs—or worse—if he doesn't get paid.

"Come on," Dad says, gesturing for me to follow him. "Why don't I give you the grand tour."

The grand tour consists of a brief stop in a galley kitchen, which is outfitted with an ancient microwave and crusty-looking counters. On to his bedroom, featuring the twin bed he took from my gran's, the one he slept in as a kid, and finally a pocket-sized bathroom, where a slimy shower curtain covered in cartoon goldfish hangs from a rusting curtain rod.

"So that's it," he says. "I know it's not much."

It certainly isn't. But I paste a smile on my face, look him dead in the eye, and lie. A talent, apparently, that runs in the family. "No, it's great. I like it."

"It's only temporary. I'll move someplace better in a few months," he says. "I'd like to be closer to work."

"You got a job?"

"Well, an interview. But I think there's real potential at this company. Room to grow."

"Dad, that's great."

I can't help but feel hopeful. Maybe this time it will be different. Maybe this time it will all work out.

"So? Shall we go out for breakfast?" Dad grabs his wallet and we head outside. It's a beautiful day, the kind of blue-sky day when it feels like nothing bad can happen.

We go to the same restaurant every weekend and it's not nearly close enough to walk to, but Dad starts down the street like that's just what we're going to do.

"Where are you going?"

"I thought we'd get some exercise," he calls over his shoulder.

"It's, like, thirty blocks! Can't we take your car?" He keeps walking and I have to run to catch up to him. "Do you need gas money or something?"

He shakes his head. "I missed a couple of payments. It's no big deal. I'll get it back."

"Are you telling me that your car was repossessed?" This has happened before, a few times actually, so I shouldn't be so shocked. But I am. I feel like I've swallowed a stone.

"Minor setback. I'll get it back soon. After I . . . pay a few other bills."

His bookie, he means.

"How much do you owe him?"

He hesitates. "Fifteen hundred dollars."

Bailing him out is enabling him. I know this. But that guy was scary.

I do a quick mental calculation. If I give him the money, it will almost clean out my savings account. The most I can earn between now and September, when I'm back at school and working fewer hours, is seven hundred dollars. And that's if I don't spend another penny all summer.

If my mom finds out I've helped him, she will kill me. But what choice do I have? He's my dad. He's in trouble and I can't stand by and do nothing. Gran would want me to help him. Besides, there's no one else left to do it.

England will have to wait.

"I can lend it to you," I say, trying to sound like I'm okay with this.

Dad's shaking his head before I've even finished the sentence. "No, ladybug. I can't ask you to do that."

I force myself to smile. "You're not asking. I'm offering." I squeeze his arm. "Dad, it's okay. It's a loan. You can pay me back."

He runs a hand through his thinning silver hair. "What about your band trip?"

"It's just a trip. England will always be there."

And in theory, that's true. England will always be there.

At this rate, I may never get to see it, but it will always be there.

The relief on his face tells me I'm making the right choice. "I promise you, Quinn, I will pay you back," he says, drawing me into a hug.

I should insist that he get help, that he learn from this mistake so it doesn't happen again. But that's all been said before, many times, by many different people. Whatever I have to say won't make a bit of difference.

We start walking again. Dad's steps are lighter and he's chatty, trying to fill the space between us with words. I half listen as he tells me about his job interview. He hasn't held down a job for any length of time in five years. Not since he worked with Wesley's mom. And look how that turned out.

The last time I saw Wesley's parents was at the going away party Gran threw for them. Mrs. James got some big-deal promotion and Wesley and his family were moving to Portland. I was miserable he was leaving and I avoided him for most of the night, figuring that, after an entire summer together, I might as well get a head start on learning to be without him.

Shortly after dinner—hamburgers on the grill, Dad's specialty—Wesley found me hiding in the apple tree in Gran's garden. He climbed up and sat beside me. The tree branch was just big enough for the two of us, but only if we sat really close to each other. I remember the roughness of the bark on the back of my legs, the smell of the not-yet-ripe apples, too bitter to eat and still small enough to fit in the center of my palm. What I could see of the sky through the leaves was purple and the stars were coming out. I caught glimpses of them twinkling like fairy lights, a million miles away. As out of reach, I thought, as Wesley would soon be.

We listened to the sounds of the party—the clink of glasses, the murmur of adult voices talking about things they wouldn't have been talking about had they known we were sitting only a few feet away. I was glad it was getting dark because I was worried I might cry, and I didn't want Wesley to see that. I had to keep reminding myself that being mad at him was pointless—it wasn't his fault he had to move—and that maybe, despite the distance, we'd still somehow remain friends.

But we didn't stay friends, obviously. Because not even five minutes later, Wesley opened his big mouth and told my mom that my dad had lost his job.

Everything bad that has happened since that night is Wesley's fault. If he hadn't said anything, my parents might have been able to work through their issues. They might even still be married. My dad wouldn't be gambling. I'd still be going to London.

All of this—everything—is Wesley's fault.

After our weekly crumpet—that I insist on paying for and, in the end, can barely eat—Dad and I walk a few blocks to the British store. It's the last place I want to be right now but I'd already told him I wanted to buy some treats for Gran. He's going to visit her today.

I could bring them to her myself, of course, but that would mean I'd have to actually go to the old folks' home we dumped her in two months ago. And I'm not ready to do that. Truthfully, I'm not sure I'll ever be ready.

Union Jack's is a specialty store that sells imported English candy and souvenirs. While Dad waits outside, I grab a wire basket and head past delicate floral teacups, a bobblehead of the queen, and commemorative tea towels of the Royal Wedding.

I have to admit, I'm tempted to buy one of them. I watched the Royal Wedding with my grandmother, right before she was diagnosed with Alzheimer's. I spent the night at her house and we got up ridiculously early to watch it live. Gran made cranberry scones and we wore fancy hats with feathers, like we were invited guests.

I stop at a long row of chocolate bars. Walnut Whip. Flake. Curly Wurlys. Because they're imported, they're, like, three bucks a bar, but they're worth every penny. I pick up a couple of Fry's Peppermint Creams—Gran's favorite—and a small bag of liquorice allsorts, these fancy pink and yellow square candies that look so much better than they taste. But Gran loves them, so I add them to my pile.

A box of shortbread, a tin of orange pekoe tea, a jar of marmalade all make their way into my basket.

I'm not even sure Gran's allowed to eat any of this stuff. According to Celia, she's on a pretty strict diet. They should let her eat whatever she wants, in my opinion. I mean, it's not like it really matters. It won't help her get better. Nothing will. So what difference are some empty calories going to make?

I bring everything up to the front. The lady behind the register puts down her copy of *Hello!* magazine and rings up my order. When I get back outside, Dad's leaning against a streetlamp, hands wedged in his pockets. His hair is messy, sticking up in tufts, like he's been working his fingers through it. I hand him the bag.

"You sure you don't want to come with me? I know she'd love to see you," he says, peeking inside.

"Some other time," I say, backing away before he can give me a hug.

Right now, I really want to be alone.

seven.

Mr. Aioki's at the podium, arms raised, when there's a knock on the band room door. I lower my clarinet, glancing around the room to see if anyone is missing, but there are no empty chairs. Everyone is here.

He stalks to the door and opens it a crack. From where I'm sitting, I can't tell who's on the other side.

Caleb rests his clarinet across his knees. "I'm surprised he answered it," he says.

So am I. As a rule, Mr. Aioki does not abide interruptions. We could be in the middle of an earthquake and he'd make us keep playing, that's how seriously he takes concert band, so it is kind of odd that he wouldn't just ignore whoever was at the door.

"Maybe he's expecting someone," I say.

A moment later the door swings fully open and Wesley James enters the room. Lugging a huge black tuba case.

This can't be happening.

Mr. Aioki grabs an extra chair and tells Wesley to squeeze between Alisha and Jiao, our brass section. Wesley smiles apologetically as the second row shuffles their seats around to accommodate him.

I'm pretty sure I'm having a heart attack. I'm all sweaty and my chest feels tight. I'm clutching my clarinet so hard the keys leave indents on the pads of my fingers.

Mr. Aioki taps his baton on the podium. "Everyone," he says. "You'll notice we have a new addition. Normally, I wouldn't accept new members into concert band this late in the year, especially this close to a tour, but Wesley James is a special case."

Oh, he's a special case all right.

I turn around to catch Erin's eye. She shakes her head sympathetically.

"Mr. James is transferring to West Seattle High in September and, as luck would have it, he plays the tuba. And as you all know, our brass section could use a bit more support."

Alisha and Jiao play the trumpet and the trombone, respectively, and they are very competitive. Like insanely so. No way will they be happy Wesley's joining their ranks.

"Let's take five to give Mr. James a chance to set up." Murmurs break out around the room as Mr. Aioki starts to shuffle through a stack of sheet music.

"Hey, man," Caleb says, turning around in his chair. Wesley plunks into the seat behind me, his tuba case knocking against the legs of my chair. "You passed the audition!"

"Yeah, I'm psyched." Wesley flips the latches on his battered case. The hinges squeak as he opens the lid.

I give him a black stare. "Why are you here?"

Wesley pulls out his tuba, his eyes narrowing thoughtfully. "You know, you ask me that a lot," he says.

That's because he's always turning up where I least expect him. He's like bedbugs: irritating and impossible to get rid of.

"You only joined because of the trip," I snap.

"Well . . . yeah," he says. "Isn't that why we're all here?"

My crazy must be showing because Caleb is giving me a strange look. Probably wondering why I'm being so hostile to his new best friend. I grab a felt cloth from my case and start furiously polishing my clarinet.

"You must be a stellar player," Caleb says. "Aioki doesn't let just anyone in."

"I'm all right," Wesley says.

I roll my eyes. Aioki wouldn't have accepted Wesley if he wasn't a better-than-all-right tuba player, no matter how much support our brass section needs. Ugh, his false modesty is gross.

Wesley tunes his instrument, his cheeks billowing as he blows a quick puff of air into the mouthpiece, oblivious to the fact that everyone in the room is sneaking looks at him. Especially the girls. Even Erin. I catch her eye and she mouths, "He is so hot."

Her reaction irritates me, although I'm not sure why. Fine, Wesley's hot. So what? Caleb's hot, too. Sort of. And a much better match for me than Wesley James.

My cheeks flush. Why am I even thinking about Wesley in that way? Being with him is not something that's ever going to happen—never, ever. The thought should make me feel sick, instead of warm all over. God, what's wrong with me?

When Wesley's finally done tuning up, Mr. Aioki steps back to the podium and we start with "America the Beautiful," a little off-key at first. I play it automatically, running through the notes without thinking, my mind on how much my life is full of suck.

I haven't told Mr. Aioki—or anyone else, for that matter—that I can't go on the tour yet. For the past few days, I've been holding out hope that Dad would find another way out of his mess, that I wouldn't need to help him, but no such luck. I gave him the money last night. So it's official. I'm not going to London.

But Wesley James is.

It's not fair.

What really gets me is that he's not even sorry about what happened between us five years ago. He hasn't even tried to apologize for ruining my life. It doesn't even matter to him.

By the time we play the first notes of Beethoven's Symphony no. 5, I'm really fuming. Wesley needs to be taught a lesson. He has to take responsibility for what he did.

And then suddenly it comes to me.

I may not be able to do anything about Wesley going to my school or being a part of concert band or even having the same circle of friends, but there is one thing I might be able to do.

Get him fired.

My mind is still buzzing, working through my plan, while Erin and I wait in line for our after-practice caffeine fix.

"Quinn? You in there?" She snaps her fingers in front of my face. "Have you heard anything I've said in the past five minutes?"

"Sorry," I say. "I was thinking."

"About Wesley?"

My cheeks redden. "Yes, but not in the way that you mean."

"Well, I wouldn't blame you if you were." Erin places our order with the barista then hands him a ten-dollar bill. For once, I don't protest when she pays. This afternoon I need the caffeine more than my pride. "He's mad cute," she says, dropping her change into the tip jar.

"Not my type."

She raises her eyebrows. "Mad cute is not your type? Since when?"

The whir of the blender keeps me from giving her an answer. We collect our drinks from the counter—two iced mochas, heavy on the whipped cream—and make our way down to the beach. As we walk on the wide cement path that lines Alki Beach, back toward Erin's house, I fill her in on my plan.

"Don't you think getting him fired is a bit harsh?" Erin says, pushing a strand of her short dark hair out of her eyes. "I mean, this all happened a thousand years ago. It's old news."

"It doesn't feel like old news to me." I move aside to avoid being flattened by a shirtless guy on Rollerblades. "A reminder: My parents would still be together if it wasn't for Wesley James. He needs to pay."

"Quinn—"

"I'm serious. And every miserable thing that's happened after they broke up is his fault, too."

"Do you hear yourself? That's insane. You can't seriously hold Wesley responsible for your parents' prob—"

"Yes I can," I cut her off. "It all stems from what he did. All of it."

Erin sighs. "Okay. But getting him fired is not going to bring your parents back together."

She's right. Of course she's right. It will not change anything and it won't make up for all the hurt. But it will make me happy. And if I can make Wesley's life even a tiny bit miserable, then it's time well spent.

"Quinn, I really think you should try to let go of this. For your own sake. It's not good to hang on to all that negative energy." She stops to dig a pebble out of her sandal. "You know what we should do? Cleanse your aura."

"My aura is fine."

"Hm. Well, it wouldn't hurt to clean it up a bit," she says. "It also wouldn't hurt to focus on something else. Or someone else."

"Like Caleb?"

"So you do like him."

I hesitate. "I like him. I'm just not sure if I *like* him like him."

"Well, we'll be in London for a whole week, barely any parental supervision," she says, dancing around me. "Perfect opportunity for some sweet band-geek love."

My heart plummets. I usually tell Erin everything, but not

being able to go on the trip? I can't even put it into words. I feel bad that I'm hiding it from her, but I don't think I can talk about it without crying yet, so I murmur, "Yeah, perfect," and listen to her run through a list of what she needs to pack and what she can buy there, until we're back at her house and she's forgotten all about Wesley and my dirty aura.

eight.

Alan leans forward on his throne, casting his gaze around the restaurant. "Heat not a furnace for your foe so hot," he says. "That it do singe yourself."

Okay, if I believed in signs, I might take that as one. Especially when Alan's eyes land on me and he slowly shakes his head, like he knows all about my evil/brilliant plan to get Wesley fired.

But I don't believe in signs. And there's no way Alan knows anything, not unless he's a mind reader. Which does not seem likely.

Still, my hands shake a little as I set the basket of bread in the middle of table six.

Alan pushes himself off his throne and continues with his

soliloquy—a single spotlight following him across the stage—while I recite the list of ingredients used in our roasted potatoes for the third time.

"Garlic, olive oil, and oregano," I say. "That's basically it."

"Basically?" The woman raises her over-plucked eyebrows. "You don't know for sure?"

My cheeks are starting to hurt from smiling at her. "No, I'm sure. That's it. Three ingredients."

She still doesn't believe me, so I tell her I'll double-check with the chef, but I don't really plan to because I already know what he'll say: garlic, olive oil, and oregano.

On my way to the kitchen, I veer behind a wide stone pillar. The perfect spot for spying on Wesley.

He's serving a group of girls who look to be about our age. One of them—a redhead in a yellow dress—is laughing a little too hard at whatever he's saying. I know from experience that nothing Wesley says is ever that funny, so I gather she must be into him. Or maybe she just has a pirate fetish.

Wesley pulls a chocolate coin from behind her ear—seriously, it's such a lame trick, I don't think it even deserves to be called a trick—and she squeals. He smiles, takes off his hat and places it over his heart, gives her a little bow. When he hands Red the coin, I catch the girl beside her rolling her eyes. This girl is the only one at the table not wearing a paper crown.

What she is wearing, however, is a very surly expression. One that tells me she'd kill to be anywhere but here.

I know the feeling.

I used to love working at Tudor Tymes. Well, maybe *love* is a strong word, but I really liked it. Tudor Tymes was my thing—no one else from school worked here. No pressure to act cool—a good thing, since that's hard to do in a medieval costume. But ever since Wesley was hired, it's been stressful. And now he's joined band and I have to share that with him as well. It's infuriating.

The very idea that Wesley James, of all people, is going on my dream trip kills me. He'll be in London, checking out Trafalgar Square, riding the London Eye, and watching the Changing the Guard at Buckingham Palace. And I will be stuck here. Forever.

The only thing that's given me any pleasure lately is my plan. I've spent most of the past week dreaming up ways to get Wesley's ass canned. As far as I can figure, my best strategy is to get customers to complain about him. As many as possible, as often as possible, until Joe has no choice but to get rid of him.

And I think Surly Girl can help me. I don't think it will take much to push her over the edge. She looks like complaining is part of her DNA.

I peek back at my table to make sure they aren't watching

for me—the last thing I need is to make my own customers angry. But the woman is busy poking distrustfully at the basket of bread while her two kids duel it out with plastic straws.

I turn back as Wesley pulls his order pad from his back pocket. This is it. Showtime.

I grab a silver pitcher from the water station and hustle over to his table. The first thing he's supposed to do is fill the guests' water goblets but, as usual, rules don't mean anything to Wesley. Something that is definitely going to work in my favor tonight.

"Need some help?" I smile, holding up the pitcher.

Wesley glances up from his order pad. He gives me a slow smile. An *I-knew-you'd-come-around-eventually* smile that makes me want to slap him. "That would be great," he says. "Thanks, Q."

I fill the girls' goblets, planning my route around the table so I end up right behind Wesley as he's taking Surly Girl's order.

"Remind me why we couldn't go for sushi?" she says to her friends.

"Aw, come on. You can have sushi anytime," Wesley says. "But eating here . . . well, this is an experience."

Surly's laser-glare is a pretty strong indication of what she thinks about this experience. And of Wesley. It occurs to me that I may not have to do anything after all. I smile. He's going to earn this complaint all by himself.

"There is nothing edible on this menu," she says.

"I don't know about that. The house special is pretty popular." He taps his pencil against the cartoon drawing of a turkey leg. "Not exactly as shown, of course."

She wrinkles her nose. "I'm a vegetarian."

Oh, this is too easy. All I have to do is change her salad order to something that used to have a face and then watch the drama unfold.

I quickly fill all the goblets, sloshing water onto the plastic tablecloth in my haste to get to the kitchen. I need to beat Wesley back there in order for this to work.

I push through the swinging door. Fortunately, it's a slow night. No one but Dean, the cook, is back here and he's too busy plating orders to notice me loitering around the computer station, but I swipe my card and pretend to place an order just in case.

A minute later, Wesley saunters in. He tosses his order pad on the desk with a sigh. "Tough crowd," he says.

"I don't know. You seemed to be making friends just fine," I say, thinking of the way the red-haired girl drooled over him.

Wesley smiles and my stomach does this weird swoopy drop.

"Jealous, Q?"

"Yes, terribly." But my cheeks suddenly feel warm. Hopefully, he doesn't notice. The last thing I need is for Wesley to think I like him. Because I don't. Obviously.

I continue punching in my fake order, very aware of how close he is.

I hate that I'm aware of how close he is.

Wesley's fiddling with his swipe card, waiting to key his own orders into the computer. I need him to turn around or talk to Dean or something so I can sneak his order pad off the desk. "I'll just be a second," I say, stalling.

"Take your time," he says. "I'm not in a hurry."

Of course not, I think irritably. *Why would you be in a hurry? You only have a table full of hungry people waiting.*

As do I. But I gave my table bread. The second thing we're supposed to do when customers arrive, as clearly outlined in our staff orientation manual. Which Wesley probably hasn't even read.

And, I realize, it's the perfect way to get him out of here so I can switch the orders.

"I noticed you haven't given table one their bread yet," I say.

"I'll take it out there in a minute," Wesley replies. "What's the rush?"

"You're supposed to give them their bread before they order," I say. "It's the rule. And do I need to remind you what happens when you break the rules?"

I let the threat of the stocks hang there. I can feel Wesley's eyes on me, but I don't look up. Finally, he sighs heavily and says, "All right, fine. Guess I'd better go and give the girls their bread before you turn me in."

He clomps off. I wait until the door swings shut before grabbing his order pad off the desk, along with a tooth-marked pencil. I carefully erase Surly Girl's order—a salad with ranch dressing on the side—then scribble "house special" in what I hope is a convincing forgery of Wesley's chicken-scratch writing. I toss the order pad back on the desk and leave the kitchen, my palms sweating.

Fifteen minutes later, after I've taken my own table's order, I'm back in the kitchen. Wesley grabs three plates from underneath the heat lamp and heads out to his table.

Bruce is behind me at the computer station. I peek through the porthole in the door, watching as Wesley sets the turkey leg in front of Surly. Her face immediately contorts, like he's placed a severed head in front of her.

"Huh," Bruce says.

Something in his voice makes me turn around. "What's up?"

"Wesley left his swipe card here." He shakes his head. "That's the second time he's just left it lying around." Wesley is disorganized, so this doesn't really surprise me. I'm thinking about how I can use this to my advantage when he shoves through the door, his face red and flustered.

Bruce hands him the swipe card and Wesley tucks it into his pocket without a second thought.

"Hey, Dean," he calls to the chef. "I messed up. I need a salad, stat." He tosses the rejected turkey leg on the counter, the platter clanking against the stainless steel.

Almost immediately, Dean slides a plate of iceberg lettuce with a few shaved carrots and two sad little tomatoes at him.

"Thanks, man," Wesley says. "You saved my butt."

Yeah, thanks, Dean.

"Wrong order?" I ask casually.

"Yeah. I wrote down turkey, and she's a vegetarian." Wesley shakes his head. "But no harm done. I managed to charm her."

Of course he did. I grimace, feeling irritated as he picks up the salad and two more platters. He leaves the kitchen, Bruce trailing behind him.

Clearly, I need to up the ante. Do something that he won't be able to easily talk his way out of. Something like . . .

I glance casually over at Dean to make sure he's not paying attention before plucking a hair out of my head. I snap it in half so it's closer to the length of Wesley's messy blond hair, then quickly stick it underneath a side of ribs. The last remaining platter destined for Wesley's table.

Okay, yes, it's a totally repulsive thing to do to some poor unsuspecting girl. The mere idea of finding a hair in my dinner gives me a whole-body shudder, but it must be done. All's fair in love and war.

I beat it out of the kitchen. I'm not paying attention to where I'm going so when I hit something that feels as solid as a brick wall, I'm knocked backward.

"Careful, lass," Alan says, reaching out to steady me. "What say you? Where are you off to in such a hurry?"

This is kind of a ridiculous question, considering we work in a restaurant. The whole point is to hustle.

"Uh, Your Highness. Hello." I bob a curtsey, my breath coming in short puffs.

Okay, so maybe Alan *is* a mind reader, because his eyes narrow, like he knows I'm up to something. Or suspects it anyway. And for Alan, raising his suspicion is enough to land you in the stocks.

"Guard!" he shouts, tightening his grip on my arm.

"No! Please," I say, trying to pull away. "I don't have time for this."

But Bruce is already coming. "What's up, Your Highness?"

"This lass is up to no good. Off to the stocks with her!"

"You know, Alan, you really don't have the authority to—"

"I'm the king of England," he roars. "Be glad that 'tis only the stocks and not the guillotine!"

Um . . . right.

Bruce disentangles me from Alan and leads me through the restaurant, to the crowd's chant of "to the stocks, to the stocks."

I keep my eyes on the ground until we pass Wesley's section. I glance up, praying he's in the back or the kitchen, and not witnessing my humiliation. But of course, he's right there. Watching me.

"Sorry, Quinn," Bruce says, gently directing my head through the wooden boards. They clap down around my neck and wrists, making my breath come even faster.

"I'll be back as soon as I can," he says.

He walks away and the chatter in the restaurant resumes as everyone quickly forgets about me. My neck's already starting to ache from the pressure of the boards and I badly need to pee.

Erin would say this is karma. Payback for getting Wesley sent to the stocks. *Maybe I do need my aura cleansed after all.*

What is already an uncomfortable situation is made infinitely worse when a pair of clunky black pirate boots enter my field of vision. Wesley bends down so I can see the sympathy in his eyes.

"Go. Away."

He stands up and rattles the board, like he's going to pull it up and get me out.

"It's no use," I say miserably. "He'll send me back in here, only for longer. I have to do the time."

The fact that Wesley's trying to rescue me makes me even more uncomfortable than being in the stocks. But one nice gesture is not going to undo everything. It won't make me forgive him. It won't make me like him.

"Get away from me!" I snap.

"All right, all right. Have it your way." But he doesn't leave. He just steps behind me.

"What are you doing?" I hiss, trying to turn around to see what he's up to. Which is impossible.

Whatever he's doing back there, he's soon got the attention of the entire restaurant. My face burns. I know it's probably just one of his stupid magic tricks, but I didn't volunteer to be part of it. Whatever it is he's doing, it must be pretty darned funny because everyone is laughing, at my expense.

I didn't think it was possible to hate Wesley James more than I already do.

nine.

As it turned out, no one complained about finding a hair in their food, which, if you think about it, is actually pretty disturbing.

My scheming may have come to nothing the other night, but I'm not ready to give up yet. There are still plenty of things I can do to get Wesley in trouble. I just need to get creative.

"If working with him is that bad, maybe you should look for another job," Erin says, squirting a blob of coconut-scented sunscreen on her arm.

"No way." I slide my red sunglasses on and settle back in the wicker lounge chair, a stack of magazines heavy on my lap. "I was there first. Wesley's the one who should quit."

We're in Erin's backyard, watching her boyfriend, Travis,

do cannonballs into her pool. It's wickedly hot. We've only been out here for a few minutes, but I'm melting already.

"Don't you think you're taking this whole revenge fantasy a bit too far?" Erin says. "I mean, what if he really needs the job?"

"He doesn't need it," I say. Not the way that I do anyway.

Erin doesn't get it. Her parents may not hand her money, but they are paying for her trip to London. Just like Wesley's will, I'm sure. The expense of two additional kids aside, his mom won't let him miss out.

Erin raises her eyebrows.

"What?"

"It's just that I've noticed—and please don't get mad at me for saying this—but it seems like he's all you talk about lately." She flips the lid on the sunscreen closed and tosses the bottle on top of the scrunched-up beach towel near her feet. "It's like you're obsessed with him."

I sit up and the magazines slide off my lap and onto the ground. "Oh my God, I am not obsessed with him! I just think he needs to be taught a lesson."

"Well, maybe he's learned it already," she says. "Maybe you should try talking to him about it."

"Erin. I don't need to talk to him. He humiliated me in front of everyone the other night." My chest tightens. Wesley apologized, claiming he thought I'd think being part of his magic act was funny—which shows just how out of touch with my feelings he is.

"Also, why are you defending him? You knew him for, like, two weeks before he moved away."

Erin sighs. "I may not know him well, but I do know you." She grabs a jumbo-sized bag of Doritos from underneath her chair and passes them to me. A peace offering. "And you are making yourself completely crazy. I just don't think it's worth it."

I guess she doesn't know me as well as she thinks she does then. Because getting revenge on Wesley? Totally worth it.

As Erin flips through the latest issue of *US Weekly*, I absentmindedly start making my way through the chips. This is the problem with chips. They are addictive and I won't stop eating them until I get a stomachache. I'm halfway through the bag when Travis climbs out of the pool. Erin's boyfriend is really good-looking, with an athlete's body.

Travis shakes the water out of his hair like a dog before ambling over and collapsing beside Erin on her lounger. "Dude, you're getting me all wet," she squeals. She shoves him and he lands with a grunt on the cement.

"Now you must pay," he says, giving her an evil grin. Erin kicks at him, but Travis moves fast. He snaps her up and throws her over his shoulder as if she's as light as a cat, and starts to walk toward the pool.

"Travis Evans, don't you dare," she says, pounding uselessly on his back with her tiny fists.

Travis obviously doesn't dare because he sets her back down on the patio and plants a kiss on the top of her head. Erin runs a finger over the tattoo of her name on his ribs, tickling him, and he twists her around so her head is stuck in his—ew!—hairy armpit. I watch them play-wrestle, wishing someone was crazy enough about me that they'd tattoo my name on their body. Even if it is a totally insane thing to do.

"Only a hundred and nineteen more days," Travis says, reaching over and yanking one of my braids.

"Ouch." I swat at him but he grabs the chips from my lap and dodges out of the way like a prizefighter.

Travis isn't in band. In fact, he isn't even in high school— he graduated last year. Despite that, he's arranged to take a week off from his construction job to come to England, so he can hang out with Erin. Since he was one of Aioki's star musicians—he plays the drums quite excellently—our band teacher had no problem with him tagging along, especially since Travis offered to be his assistant.

"I hear we're holding a car wash next weekend." Erin pulls a face.

My stomach does a nosedive. I still haven't told her that I can't go to London. I know I'll have to do it soon—we're supposed to be roommates. And as much as Mr. Aioki likes Travis, there's no way he'll let him bunk with Erin, meaning that she'll probably be stuck with Jasmine and Ashley, the other two sax players. And she can't stand Jasmine and Ashley.

She's going to kill me.

"At least he's not making us sell chocolate," I say. We had to do that one year in elementary school. I ended up eating most of them, and my mom was not happy when she had to cut a check for two hundred dollars' worth of chocolate-covered almonds.

"True." Erin picks up the sunscreen and starts reapplying. She is seriously OCD about sun damage. If she has anything to say about it, she will look seventeen forever. "So have you told your mom about the trip yet?"

"Nope." I haven't told her because she's already working double shifts to keep us in our house. If she had known about the trip, she would work herself into the grave to get me there. I can't let her do that.

"Hey, what do you guys want to do tonight?" Travis asks, brushing chip crumbs off his bare belly. "We could go to the Dragon. Practice our accents." The Elephant & Dragon is a British pub in Fremont. There's no way we'll get in.

"Quinn doesn't have an ID," Erin says.

"And you do?"

She nods. "Trav got it for me."

"I know a guy," he says.

"I can't go anyway," I say. "I have to work."

Work. Blech. Now I'm back to thinking about Wesley. I can't seem to keep him out of my brain for long. Maybe Erin's right. Maybe I am obsessed. But I feel like the only way I can put this whole mess to rest is to get him out of my life.

Which gives me a new idea. I may not be able to control whether or not a customer complains about Wesley, but if I sent someone in undercover . . .

"Actually, Travis," I say, smiling. "I need your help with something tonight."

Travis is late. I'm starting to get anxious that he's changed his mind and is backing out, but then I see Rachel leading him and his weird Scottish friend, Ewen, across the restaurant. I told Travis to ask Rachel if he could sit near the stage—Wesley's section—and sure enough, that's where she leads them.

So far, so good.

I wasn't sure I'd be able to pull this off. I had to plead with Erin for over an hour to get her to agree to let Travis do this. She finally relented because she was tired of listening to me whine. Since I couldn't send her—Wesley would recognize her—Travis brought Ewen instead.

I watch from behind the pillar as Wesley arrives at their table with a basket of bread. He sets it down on the table and

Ewen immediately attacks it. Travis, however, just stares at Wesley, eyes narrowed, arms crossed. He's doing his best to make him nervous, which is hilarious because, despite his vaguely criminal appearance, Travis is the least intimidating person ever. But that's only once you get to know him.

Wesley doesn't seem intimidated, though. He scratches their order on his notepad, gives them a friendly nod, and then heads over to the bar. He's whistling.

Not exactly the exchange I was hoping for, but it's still early in the game.

I can't help glancing over at Travis and Ewen every few minutes. I'm so distracted, I give the wrong orders to two different tables and, even worse, totally forget about some of my customers altogether until an irate lady grabs my arm as I walk past. If I'm not careful, I'll be the one getting fired.

Half an hour later, I'm in the kitchen waiting for an order of ribs when Wesley punches his way through the door, his face stormy.

"Changed their mind again," he says, tossing two turkey platters on the counter. "Turns out they really feel like salad."

My heart picks up speed. I keep my expression blank, which is a struggle because I really want to do a fist pump. "Trouble?"

Wesley glances at me. "Table ten. They've sent their order back three times. Seriously, I'm ready to kill these guys."

I've only seen Wesley lose his temper once—at the going away party, when I broke his magic wand—but I can tell he's now dangerously close to blowing his top. Travis just needs to push him a little bit more and he should go off like a rocket.

Dean pushes a couple of salad plates across the counter. "Why don't you let me take those for you," I say to Wesley. "Stay in here and take a breather."

Wesley studies me suspiciously. "Why?"

"Why what?"

"Why are you being so nice?"

My cheeks flush. "I'm always nice." Just not ever to you.

But I do feel the teensiest bit guilty as I carry the salad out to Travis's table. Which is ridiculous, because I don't have anything to feel guilty about. What I'm doing is no less than Wesley deserves.

Ewen glances up as I head toward the table. His eyes bug out at the sight of me in my corset. "Stoatin ootfit," he says.

I stare at him blankly. Ewen's Scottish accent is so thick, I need subtitles.

"Wicked costume," Travis translates through a mouthful of bread.

"Um . . . thanks." I set the small hammered-silver plates down on the table. "Whatever you guys are doing, keep doing it! It's working. Wesley's about ready to punch you."

"Are you sure about this, Quinn?" Travis says. "He seems

like a decent enough guy. What if we actually end up getting him fired? I don't know if I want to be responsible for that."

"Och aye. Ah dornt loch messin' wi' a dude's livelihood," Ewen says.

Travis nods. "It's not cool." He picks a cherry tomato from his plate and rolls it across the table. "Also, how am I supposed to eat salad without a fork?"

"You'll figure it out," I say. "And you promised to help me!"

"What am I going to say when I cross paths with him in London?" Travis asks. "He's going to remember that I'm the asshole who got him fired."

"Come on, you guys. Do me a favor and keep going, okay? Please? Please please please please please."

I don't have time to wait for his answer because the lights dim. And since Amy called in sick again, I'm stuck playing Catherine of Aragon's handmaiden. I'd rather they put me in the stocks. Performing in front of an audience—band recitals notwithstanding—is so not my thing. I feel dangerously close to throwing up as I climb the wide wooden stairs to the stage.

Fortunately, I don't have any lines. I just have to brush Julia's hair while she sits on a wooden stool and dreamily sings about her enduring love for King Henry VIII.

Alan wrote this particular act. He does that every once in a while when he gets bored with reciting Shakespeare.

I can't see much from the stage—the footlights are too

bright—which is actually a good thing. The fewer people I can see staring back at me, the better. I pick up a faux ivory–handled brush and run it through Julia's fine brown hair. She shoots me a couple of dirty looks mid-song when I accidentally pull her hair, but other than that, the act goes off without a hitch.

When the lights come up, Travis's table is empty. I catch sight of him and Ewen walking out the front door. By the time I reach them, they're already inside Ewen's dusty brown Honda.

I knock on the passenger-side window and Travis reluctantly rolls it down. "You're done already?" I say. "What happened? Did you ask to talk to the manager?"

"I couldn't do it," Travis says. "Sorry, Quinn."

"Travis!"

He rolls the window back up. Gives me the peace sign. And then they're gone in a cloud of exhaust.

The sun is just beginning to disappear but it's still warm outside—way too warm to be in a velvet costume. But I'm not quite ready to go back into the air-conditioning. I need time to think. Erin and Travis probably think I'm a horrible person with a black heart. But they don't get it. Neither of them knows what it's like to have someone shatter your family. Someone you used to consider a friend.

It's not something you ever get over.

ten.

"I guess that's it," Celia says, setting her tape gun on top of the box. That box is the last of a small stack stuffed with Gran's personal belongings. Things neither of us want but don't have the heart to get rid of. The rest of her stuff is now sitting in a thrift shop, waiting to belong to someone else. It's unbearably depressing. And it makes me wonder what Gran would think, if she knew. If she would care that her memories are being given away to strangers.

"I guess so." Looking around at the empty room gives me a stomachache, so I walk to the window and peek out at the front yard. Gran's lace curtains are gone, packed away somewhere, but her ancient venetian blinds are still in place.

Celia comes up beside me. "I should probably have someone

come and do something about the garden," she says, sighing heavily at the brown grass and dying rhododendron. "It looks awful."

My shoulders tense. This is a dig at my dad, at his complete lack of interest in keeping the place up. Even though he hasn't lived here in weeks.

Out of habit, I start to defend him—Celia did kick him out, after all—but it's hard to argue against the truth. My dad stands to benefit from the sale of the house, too, so leaving all the grunt work to us isn't fair.

"My mom probably knows someone," I say, and Celia nods. She gets along well with my mom, always has. In fact, every time she comes to town, she stays with us. Even when Gran lived here, Celia preferred our guest bedroom. She didn't want to be around my dad.

That's part of the reason I'm so protective of him. I'm the only person, aside from Gran, who's ever on his side. No one will cut him a break, especially in our family. It's like they can't see past his mistakes to who he is. They don't see the good in him anymore.

"Let's get these out to the car." She lifts a box marked FRAGILE. I packed that one, so I know it's filled with porcelain ballerinas and other knickknacks that Celia is convinced might be worth something someday.

She holds the door open with her foot while I grab a couple

of old tennis rackets and a crystal lamp that was too awkward to cram into a box. The front porch is bare—Celia hauled the wicker porch swing to the dump last week. The thought of it decaying with piles of other junk bothers me. Gran and I spent a lot of time in that swing, drinking lemonade and trading stories. The memory kicks me in the chest, and my hands start to shake. I have to tighten my grip on the lamp so I won't drop it.

Celia's rented van is parked in the driveway, the rear door open. She slides the box across the gray felt carpeting so it butts neatly against the backseat. "Just put that stuff over there," she says, gesturing to a patch of grass. "We'll put it in last."

I carefully set the lamp on the lawn, then toss the tennis rackets down beside it. I insisted on keeping them, despite the fact that the duct tape on the handles is fraying and they need to be restrung. Gran played tennis for years and there's something so depressing about getting rid of her rackets, even if they are in crappy condition and will probably continue to molder in the back of my closet.

It takes us less than ten minutes to finish loading the rest of the boxes, and then we're standing on the porch and Celia is locking the front door. My heart breaks a little. I can't believe this is the last time I'll ever be at Gran's house. All my memories of her are here. And I won't be making any new ones. At least, not any that I'll want to keep.

I still haven't been brave enough to go to see her. But the

plan is to drop everything off at the storage locker Celia rented a few miles away and then visit her at the home.

When Celia suggested that we visit Gran, I couldn't think of an excuse fast enough. I guess Celia, like my mom, figures I'll regret it later if I don't make the effort. And maybe I would. Or maybe I would be happy to not have to remember Gran the way she is now. But it seems unbelievably selfish to admit that.

"Hop in," Celia says, heading over to the driver's side. I climb in beside her and buckle my seat belt. It's grossly hot out but she won't turn on the air-conditioning—she says it's terrible for the environment, which is ironic considering she's driving a van—so I roll down the window and let the warm air rush over me.

We drive through the neighborhood, past cute little houses with flowerpots in the windows. Down Broadway and onto Madison, neither of us saying much, just listening to Willie Nelson—the only musical choice when you ride anywhere with Celia. I don't really mind. There's something comforting about his voice.

She stops in front of the industrial-looking building where what's left of Gran's life is kept behind a rolling metal door. We hop out and reverse the task, unloading the boxes into an already almost-full storage locker. It takes some creative juggling to get all the new junk stuffed inside, but we finally do, and by that time I'm cranky and hot and my shirt is sticking to me.

We climb back into the van and Celia starts to babble about Gran, how the new medication she's on makes her drowsy and not to be surprised if she doesn't seem like herself. I know she's trying to prepare me, but she shouldn't worry. I already know that Gran's not herself. She hasn't been for a long time. And in that moment, I sort of hate Celia for making me do this.

We pull into a circular driveway in front of a squat, colorless building half hidden behind a bunch of maple trees. The trees are tall and leafy and aren't letting in a lot of light. I step out of the car and it feels dark and murky, like we're lost in the middle of a forest. Which is perfect because it exactly mirrors how dark, murky, and lost I feel inside.

I'm not sure what I was expecting, but it was definitely not this. This place is so, so different from Gran's house. And not in a good way.

I know Celia feels bad enough about sticking Gran in here, so I don't want to add to her guilt by telling her how much I already hate this place. How much Gran would hate it, too, if she understood where she was. She never wanted to be a burden, but I doubt she knew what not being a burden really meant. It doesn't make me feel better to know that she's receiving the round-the-clock care that we couldn't possibly give her.

Celia walks up the cobbled path to the glass doors. I expect them to whoosh open automatically as we approach, but they stay closed until she pushes a small white buzzer mounted on the stucco wall.

"They keep the doors locked," she says. "The residents . . . sometimes they wander." It's for their own good, she adds, and I'm sure it is, but it still makes me feel like I'm visiting a prison.

The buzzer sounds and the doors slowly swing open. We step inside and the air conditioner is turned up so high it's like walking into a freezer. I guess, unlike Celia, the people who work here aren't too concerned about wrecking the environment.

The place smells weird, like Lysol and old people, and I breathe through my mouth, hoping I'll get used to it. While Celia stops to speak to the nurse behind the reception desk, I pretend to study the native art lining the lemon-yellow walls to try to calm my thundering heart.

"She's in the rec room," Celia says, taking my arm. My legs feel wobbly as she brings me down the hall, to the entrance of a narrow room. "You ready?" she asks.

I nod, even though I'm not ready. I'll never be ready.

She tugs me into the room. A handful of residents are grouped around a big-screen TV, watching some soap opera. Some of them are sitting in wheelchairs, some of them on a puffy brown couch, scrunched together like crows on a telephone line. No one pays us any attention, and I'm glad, because right now I don't want to be noticed. Celia leads me toward a wall of windows with a beautiful view of a lake. This, at least, is something good. Something to hang on to.

And then I see Gran. She's sitting in a recliner, her feet propped up. She's wearing hand-knitted slippers with little pom-poms on the toes and the fuzzy blue cardigan I got her for Christmas a few years ago. Her sparkling ruby hairpin is pinned in her white hair, right above her ear. This, at least, is familiar. My grandfather gave it to her when they were first married. It makes me happy/sad to see her wearing it. Like even though she can't remember him with her mind, maybe she still does with her heart.

"Mom?" Celia says.

Gran gives her a polite smile, the kind you give someone you don't know very well.

"I've brought Quinn with me." Celia gently pushes me forward so I'm standing in front of Gran. My lips quiver as I try to coax them into a smile. My heart suddenly feels too big for my chest and I really, really want to be anywhere but here, trying to think of something to say to the person I love best in the world, who clearly doesn't remember that she loves me best back.

I search Gran's face, hoping to find some flicker of her behind her placid expression. But there's nothing. And I know it was a mistake to come here. I should never have let Celia talk me into this. I should never have let myself hope that, by some miracle, Gran would remember me.

I shake off Celia's arm. And then I run.

I run all the way home. I stop short of going inside, though; my mom worked a night shift and I don't want to wake her up, but I also don't want to have to explain how I'm the worst granddaughter ever. I don't know if I can even talk without crying. In fact, the tears are already coming as I turn away from the front door. I decide to hide in our spider-infested shed where no one would ever think to look for me until I've calmed down. I'll probably be in there a very long time.

I'm about to walk around to the backyard when someone calls to me from across the street. In my haste to get home, I didn't notice the group of guys playing basketball in front of Ryan Anderson's house. A group of guys that includes Wesley James.

Great. Wesley is the last person I want to see me upset. I wave, hoping he'll go back to his game, but instead he takes the gesture as a sign of encouragement and jogs over, a basketball tucked under his arm. I keep my eyes on the ground so he can't see my face.

"Q?" His voice is laced with concern. "What's wrong?"

"N-nothing. I'm fine." I sniff.

"You're clearly not fine," he says gently.

I swipe at my eyes. "All right, I'm not fine."

Wesley steps toward me, like he's going to give me a hug. I back away. If he touches me, I'll completely lose what's left of my composure. I don't want to totally break down in front of him.

"Whatever it is, you might feel better if you talk about it."

"That won't make anything better," I say. "There is no better."

This is the time to tell him about Gran. I know I should—he loves her, too—but I don't. Even if I wanted to tell him, and I'm not sure that I do, I couldn't do it without ugly crying.

I'm pretty sure Wesley will only follow me if I try to make a break for the backyard, so I sit on the porch steps and take a few deep breaths.

"Wes, you coming back?" Ryan yells.

Wesley hesitates before tossing the basketball at him. "Go on without me for now," he says. Ryan shakes his head, but doesn't argue, although I can tell he's wondering why Wesley's giving up a game of hoops to talk to me.

I'm wondering that myself.

"You don't have to stay," I say as he sits down beside me.

"I know."

We watch in silence as the guys continue the game without

him. Nothing but the sound of the ball hitting the pavement and the occasional grunt or swear word. Wesley leans forward, his forearms resting on his knees. He's wearing black basketball shorts and a wrinkled blue T-shirt. He's sweaty—his shaggy blond hair is sticking to his neck—but it's the good kind of sweaty. The sexy kind of sweaty.

Wait. Why am I noticing his sweat? Why am I noticing *anything* about Wesley James? I should be focusing on my master plan to get him fired, not about how sexy he looks or whether or not he smells good.

"Remember when we used to hide out in that old apple tree in your gran's backyard?" he asks.

I pause. "Vaguely," I say. This is a lie; I remember everything about that summer, but I especially remember what happened the last time we were in the apple tree, when I almost kissed him. He wanted to kiss me, too, I know he did, but he backed away at the last second and made some stupid joke. I was humiliated and dealt with it the only way I knew how: by getting mad.

Mad enough to tell him that I was glad he was moving.

Mad enough to break his magic wand.

Shortly after that, Wesley opened his big fat mouth and blabbed to my mom about my dad losing his job, and we instantly went from friends to enemies.

That's what we are now, I remind myself.

Enemies.

"Remember when we carved our names into the bark?" he asks.

"Gran was so mad at us for wrecking her antique butter knife."

He smiles. "You mentioned she's moved?"

Without even knowing it, he's given me the opening I need to tell him Gran's in a home. But the words stick in my throat and before I can find a way to break it to him, Ryan yells, "Hey, James, quit flirting and get over here!"

Wesley shakes his head good-naturedly, but the tips of his ears start to turn red.

Flirting? Is that what Ryan thinks we're doing? Is that what *Wesley* thinks we're doing?

I am so not flirting with him.

Am I?

"You know what? I'm going to go inside," I say coldly. Let Wesley go back to playing basketball with his Neanderthal friends. He has no business being nice to me and making me feel things I shouldn't be feeling.

When I stand up, Wesley's brow wrinkles. I can see he's trying to work out what just happened. "Uh, okay," he says. "See you later?"

Unfortunately. I will never not see him because he's everywhere. And that has to change, because I just can't take it.

h hadn't met you yet and that it was a complete coincidence
was even in the restaurant." She grimaces. "I'm not thrilled
he lied. And if Wesley thinks about this for even a second,
going to put the pieces together. So can you just give up
ly?"

hy would I do that?" Sure, Wesley may have demon-
e isn't completely soulless by trying to comfort me, but
sn't get him off the hook for destroying my family.
id like him—which I don't—I wouldn't know how to
at.

about my plan, though, reminds me that I don't
ve one. I am fresh out of ideas on how to get Wesley
Erin believes I'm going to give up so easily, then
ow me as well as she thinks she does.

my arm. "You're seriously messing with your
"It would be so much more fun to forgive
ndon is supposed to be one of the most ro-
world. . . . I'll bet you won't be able to re-
we're over there."

guess now's as good of a time as any to
r going to be an easy conversation. I
n't go."

eleven.

"You ran away from your grandmother?" Erin's holding
up one of the cardboard signs she made using a whole lot of
purple glitter glue. We're standing on the sidewalk in front of a
gas station, hollering at every car that passes by—and most of
them do. We've only managed to persuade three cars into the
parking lot in the past hour. So, yeah, this fund-raiser pretty
much sucks. Like everything else in my life.

"Yeah, kind of."

"Well, it's hard, right? Seeing her like that?" Erin waves
her sign at a guy in a red convertible trapped at a stoplight. "I
mean, I get why you wouldn't want to go. I don't think I could
handle it, either."

Tears unexpectedly sting my eyes. Erin's the first person

who seems to understand where I'm coming from. My mom and Celia both think I'll regret it if I don't at least try to visit Gran again. Even my dad, the king of bad choices, thinks I was wrong for running away.

"So guess who was playing basketball at Ryan Anderson's when I got home?" I fill Erin in on my conversation with Wesley yesterday. I'm still working through what happened with him. I was superemotional, obviously, and I'm willing to admit I may have overreacted a tiny bit.

"Hm," Erin says.

"Hm what?"

She smiles. "He left his basketball game to talk to you."

"So?"

"So you think he would do that if he wasn't into you?"

"I wouldn't go that far." I shake my sign at a passing car. The kid in the passenger seat sticks his tongue out at me. I stick my tongue out back at him. "All that proves is he has some human qualities after all."

But there's a fluttering in my stomach when I remember the way Wesley looked at me yesterday. Like he really cared about my feelings. Like I mattered to him.

No one has looked at me like that for a while. Maybe not ever.

And how did I react? I shut the door in his face.

"Where is Wesley anyway?" I keep my voice ca
Erin is smart and I can never get anything past her.

"Why do you want to know?" she asks in a sin

"He's supposed to be helping us." My arms a
holding up this stupid sign. I've been here all mo
away washing cars, and I'm not even going to
doesn't even bother to show up, but he's still
I can barely stand it.

"He's babysitting his sisters," Erin says

I turn and stare at her. I wasn't really
the answer. "And you know this how?"

"Well . . ." I know Erin well, too,
making out of examining a tiny mole
she can avoid meeting my eyes. "Tra
him now." Her gaze flicks up at me,
quickly away when she catches my
you, but you're so sensitive about
Travis felt really bad about w
rant, so—"

"*Nothing* happened at the
did Travis tell Wesley tha
going to ruin everything!"

"Calm down, Wesley
crazy-ass plan. Travis t

The smile slips off her face. "Can't go where?"

"To London." The lump in my throat is so big it hurts to swallow.

"I don't understand," she says.

Neither do I, really. "I . . . don't have the money." My face burns. It is nothing short of humiliating, telling her I can't afford to go on the trip. I guess I should get used to the feeling; everyone else in band is going to find out, soon enough.

"But you've been saving all summer. You said you were almost there!"

"Yeah, well . . ."

"What did you do with all that money?"

I really, really don't want to tell her. I don't want her to know about my dad's gambling problem. I don't want anyone to know about that, ever, but Erin won't let this go without some kind of explanation. "I spent it," I say.

"You spent fifteen hundred dollars? On what?"

Quick! Quick, brain, what did I spend it on??

"Just . . . stuff. I don't know. Clothes."

She narrows her eyes, taking in my ratty old T-shirt with a map of the London Underground on it that I wear almost every other day.

"And other stuff, too. I don't know. I wasted it." God, this is the worst. From the way Erin's looking at me, it's clear she doesn't believe a word I'm saying.

"You must have *some* money left, right?"

I shake my head. I feel terrible about lying to her. I really do. But I can't tell her the truth. I just can't.

"Okay . . . well. The whole reason we're doing this car wash is to help us all get there, right?"

"We've only made a hundred dollars so far," I say. "It's nowhere near enough. Besides, that's supposed to be split between everyone."

"You can have my share."

That lump is back in my throat. I smile weakly at her, feeling like the worst friend ever. "Thanks. But it still wouldn't be enough."

"You have some time before we go. Maybe you can make it up," she says.

"There's no way I can save that much. Even if I worked night and day." I would do it, too, if it meant I could still go. "It's not possible."

"What if my mom fronted you the money? I could ask her."

"Erin, it's okay," I say. "Really. I've made peace with it." This is not even remotely true, of course. I will probably never get over not going to London.

"There has to be a way." Her face suddenly sags. "Oh my God. You know this means that I'll have to bunk with Ashley and Jasmine."

"Maybe it won't be that bad. You'll probably all end up best friends." It's my feeble attempt at a joke, to lighten the mood, but Erin doesn't laugh.

"At least tell me you blew your money on some fabulous designer bag or something," she says.

"Or something." The lie is a weight in my stomach.

"This trip will be zero fun without you."

"You'll still have Travis," I remind her.

"It's not the same. You think Travis is going to hit Oxford Street with me?"

He probably would, if she asked him. But she's right—it's not the same. I can't feel sorry for her, though, because I'm way too busy feeling sorry for myself. After all, at the end of the day, Erin is still going to England. I'm the one being left behind.

"Have you told Mr. Aioki?"

I shake my head. "I'm going to tell him soon." I haven't told him yet because there's a small part of me that's still holding out hope for a miracle.

"Maybe he'll have some ideas. I mean, you can't be the only band member who doesn't go. We're a team. Maybe they have a reserve fund for—"

"Poor people?" I say bitterly.

"That's not what I meant."

I know it's not what she meant. I shouldn't take my bad mood out on Erin. It's not her fault I can't go.

It's Wesley's.

This downward spiral my dad's been on, he wouldn't be on it if my parents were still married. And my parents would still be married if Wesley hadn't blabbed to my mom that my dad had lost his job. True, he'd lied to us and pretended to be going to work for weeks after he was fired, but still. I know we would have been able to help him with his gambling problem. Instead, everyone just gave up on him.

Fast-forward five years, and here I am standing on the side of a road, shaking a sign in front of a gas station. Not going to London.

All because of Wesley James.

So whatever delusions Erin's having about Wesley and me, that's never going to happen.

"Come on," she says, lowering her sign as the light changes and a convertible speeds past us. "It's someone else's turn to stand here and make a fool of themselves."

A few of our bandmates are gathered around a blue station wagon. The rest are standing around or sitting on overturned buckets, eating snacks from the tiny convenience store attached to the gas station. Erin hands her sign to Alisha and we head over to help finish washing the car.

Erin hands me an orange sponge she pulled out of a bucket of sketchy-looking water. "Hey, isn't that Wesley?" she says as a black Ford pickup pulls into the parking lot.

Yup, it's him. I can see his blond head through the tinted

glass. He slides out and my heart picks up speed. His head is turned my way, but the lenses of his sunglasses are so dark I can't tell if he's actually looking at me. I'm pretty sure he's about to walk over when Jasmine intercepts him. Jasmine, with her cheerleader body and long red hair and ridiculous fake eyelashes. She says something and Wesley smiles. This smile is not meant for me, but it still lights up my entire body, hitting every nerve ending and throwing my insides into a tailspin.

This is not good. In fact, it's terrible. I shouldn't be feeling anything other than deep hatred for Wesley James. But instead, I am stupidly, insanely, tremendously jealous, all because he's talking to Jasmine.

Worst joke ever, universe.

I busy myself with scrubbing the hood of the car so I don't have to watch them. Erin pats my back. I know it means she's noticed them talking, too, and that she knows it's bothering me, and that makes this whole situation infinitely worse.

A few minutes later, Wesley extricates himself from Jasmine and wanders over. "Sorry I'm late," he says. "My mom had to work. I was trapped at home with two cranky three-year-olds."

I concentrate on washing the car. I'm afraid my emotions are written all over my face, and I don't want Wesley to figure out I'm weakening. Plus, it's much easier to remember why I

hate him when I don't have to look at his ridiculously handsome face.

"How's business?" he asks.

"Not great," Erin says. "It's been slow."

I let her rattle on to him about other fund-raising ideas—a
movie night, a silent auction, a kissing booth (ew, no way!).
Erin's never been the slightest bit interested in fund-raising
before, so I know that she's holding out hope for a miracle for
me, too.

As she talks, Wesley keeps shooting glances at me, but I
ignore him and keep scrubbing at a speck of dirt on the wheel
well.

"Need some help, Q?"

"No," I say grumpily.

He crouches down beside me anyway. "Come on," he says.
"Let me do it. I feel guilty for not getting here earlier."

My hands are shaking as he takes the sponge from me. I
stand up, mostly so I can put a bit of space between us. If he
was on the moon, it wouldn't be enough space.

Erin elbows me. I know she's convinced that Wesley's offer
to help is further evidence that he likes me, but she is mistaken.
I'm not sure what is motivating him to be nice to me, especially
when I've made it clear that I'm not going to reciprocate, but
I'm positive it's not because he likes me. If he did, he wouldn't
have been so interested in what Jasmine had to say.

He can do what he likes with her. Or anyone else for that matter. I don't care.

All right, fine. Maybe I care a little.

I hate that I care. I hate *everything* right now.

And okay, I know that I just decided looking at him was a bad idea, but it's hard to turn away from the sight of the muscles in his shoulders rippling as he gently rubs the wheel well. Erin catches me staring at him and gives me a smug smile.

Stupid Wesley and his stupid muscles.

Someone turns up the music—classical, as Mr. Aioki insisted on being in charge of the playlist. Another car drives in. I don't love washing cars, but I love standing next to Wesley James even less, so I walk over.

"Hey, Quinn," Caleb says, smiling as I approach. His khaki shorts and T-shirt are damp with suds and his normally perfectly coiffed brown hair is messy. I'm not used to seeing Caleb anything other than put together. I like this ruffled side of him.

"Is it weird seeing Wesley driving around in your truck?" I ask him.

"A little bit, yeah," he says. "But it's all right. He's a good dude."

"If you say so," I say. I just walked away from Wesley so I didn't have to be near him and now here I am, bringing him up.

Caleb's eyes widen. "You don't like Wes?" He says this like he can't imagine anyone not liking Wesley James. Which just proves that Wesley's grossly fake personality has fooled everyone in the world except for me.

But given that Caleb is friends with Wesley, I'm not entirely sure how he'll take me disparaging him, so I just shrug and say, "He's all right."

Caleb studies me for a moment. Then he leans over and brushes a strand of hair out of my eyes. The gesture is so unexpected that the smile freezes on my face. I'm simultaneously worried that he's going to try to kiss me, right here in front of everyone, or that he won't try at all and I've somehow read him completely wrong.

And here's the problem: I don't know if I want Caleb to kiss me. I thought I did, but then Wesley came back to town and my focus shifted from deciding whether or not to go for Caleb to getting revenge on Wesley James.

"I guess we should finish up," Caleb says.

I nod.

An hour later, I'm no closer to figuring anything out. I'm exhausted and my clothes are completely soaked. We've raised another sixty dollars, including the wrinkled twenty that Wesley pulls from behind Erin's ear.

"I guess that's a wrap," he says, stuffing the money into the converted Kleenex box we're using as a cash register.

"I guess so," Erin says. "Hey, a bunch of us are going back to my place—"

I whip my head around and give her an evil glare. I cannot believe she's about to invite him back to her house. What is wrong with her?

"Uh," she says, faltering.

An awkward silence descends. Wesley looks back and forth between us, but he clearly gets the message because he says, "Thanks, but I've got some errands I need to run." He holds up the box. "I'll just take this over to Mr. Aioki."

Erin waits until he's out of earshot before she says, "What was that?"

"What?"

"You could have let him come."

"I don't want him to come."

"Yeah, that was obvious," she says. "You're being insane, you know that, right? This vendetta or whatever it is, it's just so silly."

"It's not, actually," I say coldly. There's nothing silly about it.

"Quinn, I know you think he's responsible for your parents' divorce, but—"

"No but. He *is* responsible."

"Okay, fine. But hating on him . . . it kinda makes things difficult for the rest of us." She hesitates, and I can see she's weighing her words. "You know Travis is having a party on Saturday."

I cross my arms. "Please tell me you didn't invite Wesley."

"Honestly, I didn't think it was such a big deal," she says. "And don't say you're not coming, because you are."

Three weeks ago, no one in Seattle remembered Wesley James even existed, aside from me. And now he's completely infiltrated my life and somehow managed to brainwash my friends.

"Oh, I'll be there," I say. I have to go so I can reverse the damage and show them what a tool bag he really is.

twelve.

"Notice anything different?" Rachel asks, leaning close so I can see the small gold stud in her nose.

"Shut up! You got your nose pierced? Has Joe seen it yet?"

Rachel shakes her head.

"He's going to freak." Joe's always harping about authenticity. Girls in the fifteen hundreds did not pierce their noses. Or any other body parts, except for maybe their ears, and I'm not even sure they did that.

She shrugs. "What's he going to do? Fire me? There are laws against that." But she checks over her shoulder to make sure he's not lurking behind her.

She's right: There are laws against unjustly firing someone.

Which means I have to make sure that my plan to get Wesley canned is airtight.

Not that I have a plan. It's been two days since the car wash and I still haven't thought of a way to get him fired. And I have to do it soon, because my resolve is weakening. Every time I see him, he chips away a little more at my defenses, and I'm afraid if I spend much more time with him, they'll crumble completely. That can't happen.

The restaurant doesn't open for another half an hour, so Rachel's showing me a photo of the exact shade of blue she wants to dye her hair when Wesley comes charging through the front door.

What is he doing here? His shift doesn't start for another hour. I *may* have checked his schedule, but only so he wouldn't catch me off guard. Like he's doing right now.

He's dressed in his pirate costume—billowy white shirt, black leather vest, big black boots with the laces undone. His skull and crossbones hat is clenched in his fist and there's a distinctly un-Wesley-like scowl on his face—an expression that only darkens when his eyes land on me.

Uh-oh.

"Can I talk to you?" His voice is tight. He glances at Rachel leaning on the hostess desk, watching us with interest. "In private," he says.

I do not want to talk to him in private, now or ever, but he turns on his heel and stalks down the hall. I'm not sure what he could be so worked up about, but unless I want him to air his issue in front of Rachel—the gossipiest person ever—then I have no choice but to follow him.

My heart hammers as I walk toward the little alcove I just saw him disappear into. Wesley rarely gets mad. At least, the Wesley I knew five years ago never did. But I've done a few things lately that might make him angry, so it's difficult to know exactly what set him off.

I guess I'm about to find out.

I find him sitting on a stone bench underneath a portrait of a glowering King Henry VIII. Henry looks a lot happier to see me than Wesley does. Wesley's arms are crossed over his chest. His posture isn't superinviting, but I sit beside him because there isn't anywhere else to sit and I'd feel even more awkward standing in front of him. The bench is cold and hard, but it's nowhere near as uncomfortable as the lengthening silence between us.

"When were you going to tell me about Gran?" he finally says.

My breath catches. Of all the things I expected he might say, this wasn't one of them.

Wesley stares at me and his eyes are so full of anger and

hurt, I have to look away. "You knew I wanted to see her," he says. "You didn't think you should tell me that she has Alzheimer's?"

"How . . . ?"

"I wasn't getting anywhere with you, so I called your house. Your aunt filled me in."

Thanks, Celia.

"I can't believe you didn't tell me," he says.

A spark of anger ignites inside me. Who does he think he is? "I didn't realize I had to," I say. "She's my grandmother. Not yours."

It's a mean thing to say, and I regret it as soon as it's out of my mouth. I know Wesley loves Gran and I know she loves him, too. I also know she wouldn't be at all happy about the way I'm treating him. No matter what my reasons.

"Sorry. I shouldn't have said that." I can't believe I'm apologizing to Wesley James. But Gran would want me to be kind, and it's the least I can do for her. And also because he's right: I should have told him. Despite everything, he deserved to know.

Wesley's breathing changes. Slows down. His face softens, the lines in his forehead smooth out. He lets out a long breath and leans forward, rests his elbows on his knees. I'm relieved he's no longer mad, even though he has every right to be.

"This sucks," he says.

"Yeah."

"How long has she been sick?"

"Awhile."

He fiddles with his hat, pulling at a loose thread at the top of the embroidered skull. "I figured something was up. The last package I got from her was about six months ago."

I still can't believe Gran kept in touch with him and never said a word to me about it. I didn't keep secrets from her. But she sure kept a big one from me.

"What was in it?"

"The usual stuff," he says. "A couple of comic books, some of her shortbread cookies. A letter."

I swallow. Now is the time to tell him that I have a bundle of letters he wrote to her. I found them the other day in one of the boxes of Gran's stuff that Celia and I packed. Not gonna lie, I was tempted to read them. So very tempted. But in the end I decided not to because I know Gran would have been seriously disappointed in me. And I have enough guilt when it comes to her.

I should tell Wesley I have his letters. I should, but for whatever reason, I don't.

"I wrote her to tell her that we were moving back to Seattle," he says. "I was a bit nervous about coming back here." He glances at me. "I didn't know what to expect, if anyone would be happy to see me."

By anyone, he obviously means me. And that makes me

wonder what Gran told him about my life. How much of what's happened in the past few years does Wesley know about?

"I guess that's why she didn't answer my last letter," he says.

There's a sinking feeling in my stomach as I think about him waiting for an answer, waiting for Gran to respond.

"She didn't want anyone to know she was sick," I say.

She was diagnosed a couple of years ago, but it was only about six months ago, right around the time she must have sent Wesley her last letter, that she finally told me.

I'd seen a change in her over the past couple of years, of course—she'd forget simple things, like the name of the street she lived on or where she'd put her keys—but I didn't think anything was really wrong with her. I just thought it was a normal part of growing older.

My gran seemed indestructible. She'd always been there and I assumed she would be for a long, long time. Until I no longer needed her, anyway. Not that I could imagine not ever needing her.

The worst part? I would have noticed she was sick a lot sooner if I wasn't so wrapped up in my own life. That last year, I didn't see her nearly as much as I should have. I was too busy, I always had something else—something better—to do.

I can never get that time back. I can't make it up to her.

And knowing that, having to live with that, hurts more than anything.

Wesley leans back against the fake stone wall. He clears his throat. "Maybe we can visit her together."

I've heard when an animal, like a fox or a wolf, is caught in a steel trap, that it will do anything to get away, even chew off its own leg. That's how I feel right now. Like I would chew off my own leg to get away from this conversation.

"There's really no point," I say. "She won't remember you."

He shakes his head. "That doesn't mean there's no point, Q."

Easy for him to say. He hasn't seen her. He doesn't know what it's like to sit across from someone you love and have them look at you like you're a stranger.

Wesley must see the fear on my face because he says, "If you want me to, I'll go with you."

And just like that, another piece of the wall I've built up between us crumbles. It suddenly occurs to me that no matter what happened between us in the past, like it or not, Wesley and I are connected by our love for Gran. By our memories of her. And right now, it feels like he might just be the only person who understands what I'm going through. Because he's going through it, too. Maybe not to quite the same degree as I am, but he is.

Wesley's hand is resting near mine, close enough that if I just moved an inch or two, we'd be touching. A sense of longing suddenly sweeps through me, so strong that it scares me. My feelings for him are all over the place. They shouldn't be, but they are, and I don't know what to do about them.

I know what Erin would say: Take his hand. Take his hand and let go of everything. He can help you through this. You can get through it together.

I'm so close to doing that when I hear the solid tread of boots slowly coming down the hall. Heavy breathing. The tap of a cane against the stone floor.

Wesley and I exchange an uneasy glance. By unspoken agreement, neither of us says anything as the footsteps draw closer. Maybe if we're quiet, if we're really lucky, Alan will pass right by us.

I hold my breath as he lumbers past. But just when I think we're in the clear and we've escaped his notice, Alan stops and turns around.

"Well, well, well," he says, stepping into the alcove. He's so large, he blocks the entrance. "What have we here?"

"Hi, Alan," Wesley says. "Can you give us a minute?"

I elbow him. Clearly, he's forgotten what happens when you provoke the king. I do not want to end up in the stocks again.

"Good afternoon, Your Majesty," I say. I would curtsey,

but with Alan towering over us, there's not enough room to stand up.

Alan strokes his beard, studying us. He's dressed in a black tunic and a long purple cape, a brassy gold crown with fake rubies perched on his head.

"Lovers' quarrel?" he asks.

Wesley flushes a deep red. I feel my own cheeks burning.

Alan clearly doesn't pick up on our utter mortification. Because if he did, I'm sure he wouldn't do what he does next: close his eyes and start to sing, low and deep and slightly off-key. *"Pastime with good company. I love and shall, until I die. Grudge who list, but none deny! So God be pleased, thus live will I."*

I have no idea what the lyrics mean, but I'm guessing from the wide smile he gives us when he's finished that it's some sort of love song.

"I wrote that in 1513 for my beloved Catherine," he says.

"Didn't you behead her?" Wesley says.

I elbow him again.

"I did not," Alan says indignantly. "I had our marriage annulled. I needed a male heir, you see." He suddenly straightens, a signal that he's gearing up to give us a full report on King Henry VIII's extremely colorful love life.

"Apologies, Your Majesty, but I must finish preparing for the royal banquet," I say. "Your guests are set to arrive forthwith."

Alan rubs his hands together eagerly. "I hear we are having quite the feast!"

Really, it's the same old turkey legs we serve every night, but I can't help but admire his enthusiasm.

Before I can stand up, Wesley lightly grabs my elbow.

"Can you wait for me when your shift ends?" he whispers. "I'll give you a ride home."

I know he's probably only offering to give me a lift because he wants to continue our conversation, to talk more about Gran and try to convince me to go see her with him, and not because he's actually into me. But while my head understands this, my heart can't seem to tell the difference; it's beating double time, so quickly I feel light-headed.

Spending more time with Wesley is the last thing I should be doing. And yet I find myself telling him yes.

It's weird being in Caleb's truck without Caleb. Nothing's changed, really, except for the rabbit-popping-out-of-a-top-hat thingy hanging from the rearview mirror. But it feels different in here. Smaller, somehow. Wesley fills up the space more. Or maybe I'm just more aware of him than I ever was of Caleb.

I move closer to the door to put as much room between us as possible. But the distance doesn't really help. I'm still way too aware of him.

"I can't tell you how nice it is to drive something that's not covered in Goldfish crackers," Wesley says, backing out of the parking space.

"Hm." I fiddle with the radio until I find a country station. I hide a smile as he glances over at me, one eyebrow raised.

"Really?" he says. "You like country music?"

"Shows what you know. I've always liked country music."

He's clearly not convinced, but he doesn't switch the station. At a stoplight, he lifts his pirate shirt and sniffs the hem, exposing a swath of his tight, flat stomach and a fine trail of golden hair that makes me warm all over. He makes a face. "God, I stink," he says.

He smells, it's true, but underneath the fried turkey there's something else, something distinctly Wesley that makes my knees start to shake.

It's only pheromones, I tell myself. Just a simple chemical reaction. It doesn't mean anything.

But Wesley chooses that moment to smile at me—a real smile, not his usual irritating smirk—and my stomach does a slow cartwheel.

He's always been pretty easy to read—at least, the Wesley I used to know was—but I can't tell what that smile means, or what's going through his mind right now. Or maybe I've just lost the ability to read him.

We drive the rest of the way to my house in silence. Even

though I tell myself not to, I keep stealing glances at him. His window is rolled down and the wind is ruffling his blond hair. I like his profile. His nose isn't perfect, it's a little too big for his face, and his ears stick out, which is why he wears his hair long. But put all together, he is devastating.

The scale is seriously beginning to tip in his favor. All because he's good-looking! I am so shallow.

Wesley must feel me watching him because he takes his eyes off the road for a second and looks over at me.

"So I have an idea," he says. "Maybe when we're in London, we can check out your gran's old house. Remember all those stories she used to tell us?"

My smile falters. London. Right.

When I don't answer him right away, he glances at me again. "You don't seem excited. I was expecting excitement."

"Well . . . I definitely want to see where Gran grew up."

Someday.

"I sense a but . . ."

But I'm not going to London.

I don't say it, though. I don't want to tell him. Not yet. We've done enough deep diving in my emotions today.

"What aren't you telling me?" he asks.

So I may not be able to read Wesley anymore, but it appears that he can still read me.

I shake my head. "It's nothing."

I don't think he believes me, but he's run out of time for questions because we're now in my driveway. He glances at our house.

"The place looks pretty much the same," he says.

Maybe it's the same on the outside, but the inside has definitely changed.

"Thanks for the ride," I say, climbing out of the truck.

"Hey, Q?" Wesley calls out the window. "I meant what I said. I'll go visit her with you, if you like." He sounds so sincere, so willing to help, that it further disarms me.

Hating Wesley James is becoming increasingly difficult. My judgment is being clouded by his hot looks and his general niceness.

"Thanks," I say. But there's no way I'm taking him up on that.

thirteen.

Dad waits until I've almost finished my breakfast before dropping his bombshell.

"I don't understand," I say, blinking at him. I set my fork on the plate, my appetite obliterated. "You said you needed that money to pay off your bookie."

"Yes, well, that was the plan." The smile hasn't slipped from his face, but he won't meet my eyes. "But then I got a tip on a horse. A sure thing."

I do not like where this story is going. Not at all. "There's no such thing."

Dad rips open a packet of sugar and dumps it into his coffee cup. He picks up a spoon and starts to methodically stir, using the distraction to gather his thoughts. "The thing is, ladybug, I really believed that I could double our investment," he says. "I was sure I'd make enough to pay him off and send you on your trip."

There is a small corner of my heart that is hoping—praying—that he's going to tell me he came through this time. That he's not going to say he lost all my money on a stupid bet. "And?"

He grimaces. "And . . . well. Turns out Irish Whiskey wasn't such a sure thing after all." He finally meets my eyes and, with that, the last bit of hope I had of getting to London is gone.

How could I be so stupid? I gave him all of my money. I gave him my dream. And for what? So he could gamble it away on a horse?

The worst part is, I should have known better. I've seen what he's done to my mom, to Celia. Even to my gran. I just didn't think he'd ever do it to me.

"I can't believe this."

"Ladybug, I know you're upset," he says, reaching for my hand. "But I will pay you back. This is a minor setback. I've had a streak of bad luck, that's all. Gambling is all about odds—it'll turn around. I just need to catch a break."

I'm going to throw up. Right in the middle of this restaurant.

"I'll make it back. I always do," he says.

Not true. Not even close to being true.

"So what now?" I shake his hand off. "What about your bookie? How are you going to pay him? He doesn't exactly look like a patient person."

"Keep your voice down." Dad glances at the couple at the table next to us. They're staring at their menus, pointedly trying not to eavesdrop. "I told you, I'll figure it out," he whispers. "Trust me."

Trust him? That's all I've ever done. And look where it's gotten me.

"What about your job interview?" If he got the job, maybe he could make enough to pay me back. Please God.

He flinches. "Yeah, that didn't work out, unfortunately."

Of course it didn't.

I push my chair back and grab my messenger bag from underneath the table. "I have to go."

"Quinn, please," he says. "I know you're disappointed you're not going to London, but—"

"Yeah, I am. Of course I am. But that is nothing compared to how disappointed I am in you." I don't stay to see if my words have any impact—why would they? He's heard the same thing from the rest of my family, many, many times before—I push through the door and out onto First Street.

I cross the street and head to Pike Place Market, where

I can easily get lost. The market is especially busy on Saturdays, and I know a spot that Dad would never think to look for me. I slip past a knot of tourists who are watching the guys behind the famous fish counter toss fish at one another. Down the stairs, until I'm standing in a crowded alley that smells like watermelon and fruit punch, thanks to the million pieces of gum covering the red brick walls and hanging from the grimy windows like stalactites.

The Gum Wall is a local landmark, started in the early nineties, who knows why. It's totally gross, but strangely fascinating. For reasons I can't even explain, I find myself dropping by whenever I'm in the neighborhood. I can't leave without contributing to the wall—I feel like it's bad luck or something, and God knows I don't need any more of that—so I dig a piece of Juicy Fruit out of my bag.

While I'm chewing the flavor out of the gum, a couple in matching fanny packs and visors asks me to take their photo. After months working at a theme restaurant, I'm so conditioned to snapping photos for strangers that I automatically take their camera when the woman shoves it at me, when all I really want is to be left alone.

"Oh, are you from England, honey?" the woman asks, pointing at my Union Jack T-shirt.

Note to self: Get rid of all British souvenir T-shirts. Of

course, this will mean dumping a hefty chunk of my wardrobe as well as my personal style, but it will be worth it if I don't have to answer such painful questions.

"Nope. I grew up here." In Seattle, obviously. Not right here at the Gum Wall. But I'm sure she gets that.

"Well, it's a lovely city," the woman says as I pose her and her husband underneath a huge pink gum heart. "We're so excited to be here. We came all the way from Cleveland."

It's weird to think of Seattle as someone's dream, the same way that London is mine. The Gum Wall could totally be this lady's Buckingham Palace.

So, after I hand her back her camera, I muster up a smile and give her a list of places to visit. Less touristy places, the kind of inside scoop you can really only get from a local. The type of places I'd want someone to tell me about if I was visiting the city for the first time.

Hopefully, someone will do the same thing for me when I finally get to London one day.

Travis and Ewen's apartment is near the beach. And that's about the only good thing I can say about a place that belongs to two boys with no interest in domestic chores. I would wager that neither of them has cleaned the bathroom since they moved in six months ago. It's so bad that I refuse to use their toilet. If the situation gets dire tonight—and it might, considering that I'm already on my second beer—I'll use the gas station down the street. Where I have less chance of catching something.

I'm sitting on the lumpy futon Travis rescued from a thrift shop, hoping the alcohol will make me feel better. I don't even really like beer, but I need something to help me relax. I'm a total ball of tension. So far, it's not really helping, but maybe I just need to drink more.

Wesley isn't here yet. Every time the door opens, I expect it's going to be him. Every time it's not, I take another swig of beer. The waiting is killing me. I don't want him to come, but at the same time I've been waiting for him to arrive all night.

Ewen sets down an ice cream bucket filled with Doritos on the overturned plastic crate that functions as their coffee table.

"Haur ye gang," he says, then walks away.

I'm about to reach for a handful of chips when Erin stops me with a shake of her head. "I wouldn't recommend it," she says. "Trust me. The things I've seen them do with food . . ."

I pull my hand back. She doesn't need to elaborate. I probably should have known better. See: unholy state of their bathroom.

Travis is across the room, fiddling with the dial on his enormous stereo system. It makes zero sense that two guys living in virtual poverty should own such an elaborate and obviously expensive piece of audio equipment. Clearly, music is higher up on the list of priorities than decent furniture.

"Is anybody else coming?" I ask, picking at the label on my beer bottle. I don't look at Erin. I don't want her to know that I'm asking about anyone in particular, but she figures it out anyway.

"If you're referring to Wesley, he's coming with Caleb."

A flush creeps up my neck and into my cheeks. "Actually, I was wondering about Caleb."

It's better if she thinks I'm into Caleb. I don't want her thinking I like Wesley. If I admit I might be having non-hate-y feelings for Wesley, then she'll pressure me to do something about it. Or, at the very least, try again to talk me out of my quest to get him fired.

By the time he finally shows up an hour—and two more beers—later, I'm pretty buzzed. Enough not to be too bothered when he's quickly surrounded by my friends, people he hasn't seen since grade school but with whom he seems to fit right in.

I'm trying for cool indifference by pretending that I haven't seen him, that I haven't been watching the door all night, but Erin swiftly shatters my cool with an elbow to my ribs.

"Wesley's totally sneaking looks at you," she whispers.

"You're drunk."

"Okay, yes. But that doesn't change the fact that he keeps staring at you."

"Maybe he's staring at you," I say, but my heart seizes.

"I guess we're about to find out," she says. "He's coming over."

I glance up and, sure enough, Wesley's making his way toward us. Erin shoots me a look—*see?*—as she makes room for him on the couch. He plunks down, squeezing between us.

I slide my eyes at him. He's sitting uncomfortably close, his leg brushing against mine. The zing that goes through me, well, I'll just ignore that.

"We were wondering where you guys were," Erin says.

I scowl at her. I don't want Wesley to know we were discussing him.

"Oh yeah?" Wesley smiles at me and there's that zing again. Stupid zing.

"I wasn't wondering where you were," I say. Which, of course, makes me sound like a complete maniac. Even more so because I'm slurring my words.

He takes in the beer bottle in my hands, the bits of shredded label littering my lap. "Q . . . are you drunk?"

For some reason, I find this funny, so I start to laugh. And I can't seem to stop.

"I guess that answers my question," Wesley says as hysterical tears run down my face. It all stops pretty suddenly, though, when I'm hit by a really strong desire to throw up.

Wesley must notice that I've turned green because he takes my bottle and passes it to Erin. "Why don't we get you some air." He stands up and grabs my hand, helps me to my feet. The room spins. I'm so busy trying to keep everything down that I barely register when he slides his arm around my waist. I let him lead me outside onto the tiny balcony. He slides the grimy glass door closed behind us, cutting us off from the party and the throbbing techno music. We're on the third floor but it feels much higher, maybe because the stars are so dizzyingly close, like I could touch them if I just reached high enough.

Wesley steers me to a weathered lawn chair parked beside a planter full of cigarette butts. Judging from the sheer amount of butts—and the pyramid of empty beer cans stacked in the corner—Travis and Ewen spend a lot of time out here.

That planter, I decide, is my backup plan. While throwing up in front of Wesley would be beyond humiliating, I still feel like it's a better option than that bathroom. Fortunately, the cool night air has already started to calm my stomach, so maybe I'm out of the woods.

Wesley leans against the rusted wrought iron railing, studying me as I take deep breaths, like I'm practicing yoga. "Better?" he asks.

I nod. "A bit, yeah."

He glances up at the fat yellow moon. Since he's no longer looking at me, I feel safe studying him. I'm so used to seeing him in his pirate costume that he looks kind of weird in normal clothes. Less like he should be on the cover of a romance novel, and more regular hot boy. He's wearing faded jeans and a gray T-shirt the same stormy color as his eyes.

What is *wrong* with me? Wesley James ruined my family. I'm going to give up hating him just because he's all right to look at and he makes my knees a little bit weak?

Pathetic.

It's then that I notice something crawling along the dirty cement, near Wesley's foot. It's a big nightmare of a spider—ugly and hairy, probably it has fangs—and I'm totally paralyzed. When Wesley sees it, he bends down, extends his fingers, and lets the thing *crawl into his hand*. Then he gently moves it to the railing where it won't get stepped on.

He catches the horrified expression on my face and smirks. "Come on, Q. You're not scared of a little spider, are you?" He makes a move to pick it up again and I get a little scream-y. He chuckles. "I'm just messing with you."

Of course he is. He's always messing with me. He's made it his life's work to mess with me.

"I'm not that surprised that you're afraid of it, actually," he says.

"What does that mean?"

"You seem to be afraid of a lot of things."

My eyes narrow. *Oh my God. Who does he think he is?*

"Elaborate," I say. *Before I kick you in the junk.*

"Let's see . . ." Wesley strokes his chin, his eyes wandering the sky, like he's searching for the answer up there. "Clowns."

I snort. "So? Everyone is afraid of clowns. If you aren't afraid of them then there's something wrong with you."

"I'm not afraid of them," he says.

"And you just proved my point."

He smiles. "All right then. Thunder. Remember that time we got caught in a storm?"

Yes, I do. We were on the way home from school. I made him run the entire three miles, even when my lungs felt like they were going to burst after the first couple of blocks. By the time we got to our street, I was soaked to the skin, but so relieved to be home, I hardly cared.

The other thing I remember about that day? Wesley held my hand the whole way. I didn't have to ask him to do it; he just did.

"Big deal. Those are totally common, everyday fears," I say. "It's not like I'm afraid of things that actually matter."

A total lie, obviously. I'm afraid to see Gran and that matters more than anything else. But I'm definitely not going to tell him that.

Maybe it's the alcohol—okay, it's definitely the alcohol—but suddenly I want to prove to Wesley that I'm not afraid of anything. Not him, and not a little spider. So I get out of the chair and, without really thinking it through, grab the spider off the balcony railing.

OhmyGodohmyGodohmyGod. It is hairy. And crawly—*oh so very crawly*. I really want to shot put it over the side of the balcony, but if I show fear, that will prove Wesley's point. And I'm so not doing that. So I let this spider crawl on my hand, trying to ignore the tickling sensation on my palm. It's almost worth it just to see the shocked expression on Wesley's face. Almost.

After what seems like forever but is probably only ten seconds or so, I set the spider back down. I am dying to go to the gas station and scrub my hands, maybe throw up a little, but I lean against the railing to steady my shaking legs.

"Well," Wesley says. "I did not expect that."

I shrug like it's no big deal, even though it totally is. I held a spider! There is nothing I can't do.

"So now we just have to work through your clown issues. Maybe we should go to the circus sometime," he says. He's suddenly standing close to me. Way too close. Like if he took one step forward, we'd be sharing the same breath. One small step closer and he could kiss me.

For the first time since Wesley James walked back into my

life, I'm not thinking about how to get him out of it. I'm thinking about kissing him.

I lean into him a little and his mouth curves into a smile, like he knows what I'm thinking. Because he's thinking the exact same thing.

My heart is full-on racing now.

But as his fingers skate lightly over my arm, sending zings through my entire body, someone raps on the door. A blond girl is standing on the other side of the glass. When Wesley looks over at her, she smiles.

"Do you know her?"

"Uh, yeah," Wesley says, taking a step away from me. "That's Jolie. My girlfriend."

fourteen.

Whatever it was that was about to happen between Wesley and me—if anything was about to happen—vanishes as the girl slides open the glass door and bounces onto the deck.

Wesley has a girlfriend. A GIRLFRIEND! One that he's never mentioned. Although, since I've made a point of not asking him any personal questions, this shouldn't really come as a surprise.

Still. I am struck by how much it bothers me. It should not bother me. But oh, it does. Especially when this girl slides into the space I just vacated and wraps her arms around his waist. Something she does with ease, probably because she's done it a million times before.

"Hey, you," she says, standing on her tiptoes to give him a kiss. "I know we agreed I wouldn't come up for another few weeks, but I just missed you so much."

"Uh, hey." The tips of Wesley's ears have turned red. He shoots me a look that I can't quite decipher. Probably it's pity. Pity for me for thinking, even for an instant, that there could ever be anything between us. "Quinn, this is Jolie," he says.

"Nice to meet you." She smiles. She is Tinker Bell in combat boots—short, pixie-cut blond hair, wide blue eyes, perfect little snub nose. She's wearing baggy cargo shorts that hang off her hips, a snug T-shirt, and beat-up black boots that somehow make my red flip-flops with cherries at the toes seem tragically uncool. But they're one of the only non-British-y items of clothing I haven't gotten rid of.

"Jolie is from Portland," he says.

"We're doing the long-distance thing." She rests her cheek against his chest in a way that makes me want to break her tiny fairy arms off.

This is not good. Not good at all. I feel sick and I don't think it's just the alcohol. Somehow, against my better judgment, I've developed serious feelings for Wesley. HOW DID THIS HAPPEN?

My face feels unnaturally stiff. I'm trying to return her smile, but my lips aren't fully cooperating. I must have some weird smile/frown hybrid going on because Wesley seems kind of alarmed. He clears his throat and turns his attention back to his girlfriend.

"How did you know I was here?" he asks her.

She gives him a gentle punch to the ribs. "You weren't answering your phone, so I called Caleb. He gave me the address." She gazes up at him, smiling slyly. "Surprised?"

He nods. So I guess that makes two of us.

Wait. She knows Caleb? I guess that means she's visited Wesley before. Met his friends. Probably stayed with his family.

As if to underscore their relationship, Jolie kisses him again. Only this time, she puts a whole lot of feeling into it. Enough that a blush creeps into my cheeks, as if I'm spying on a very private moment. Which I guess I sort of am.

It's clear that I'm cramping their reunion and I definitely don't want to stick around until they finally get tired of tonguing each other, so I squeeze past them to get to the door. But in my haste, I trip over the planter and send cigarette butts flying all over the artificial turf.

"Whoops," I say, laughing a little. What I really want to do is curse because I stubbed my toe hard against the ceramic pot. "Guess I'm still drunk." And I am, a little bit, although not enough to forget that this ever happened, unfortunately. "Nice to meet you," I say to Jolie.

"Yeah, you too." She doesn't look at me when she says this, but then, she's distracted—her hand has found its way underneath Wesley's T-shirt. I hear her say, "What did you say her name was again?" as I slide the door closed.

Erin's still sitting on the couch, but Travis is with her now, and since the last thing I want is to be with another happy couple, I pretend not to hear her calling my name. Instead, I limp into the kitchen where I find Caleb standing in the corner, his hands tucked into his pockets. He looks as uncomfortable as I feel.

"Hey," he says, watching me dig my bag out from the jumbled pile underneath the kitchen table. "You leaving?"

"Yeah. I need to take a walk," I say.

"Want some company?"

I should say no. I should go home and calm down, remind myself of all the reasons why I should still hate Wesley James. Why I should still destroy him. But maybe that's not what I need right now. Maybe what I need is a distraction from this terrible, terrible day. A distraction, perhaps, in the form of my very cute band partner.

"Sure." I slide my bag over my shoulders. Caleb follows me out the door and we head down the hall. I have no real destination in mind, but my feet eventually lead us toward the beach. He's chatting about England, all the places he wants to see. I've never heard him sound so excited.

I wish he would stop talking.

"We should check out the Globe Theatre one night," he says. "You know, where Shakespeare put on his plays?"

"I'm kind of burnt out on Shakespeare, to be honest." I get enough of him at work. And it's not like I'll be in England to visit the Globe anyway. "But you should definitely check it out."

"Yeah, maybe," he says. We walk past the restaurants and little souvenir shops that line the boardwalk, then cut across the street. At this time of night, the beach is pretty much deserted. As we get closer to the water, the air cools down, enough that I wish I'd worn more than just a T-shirt.

I sit down on the sand and kick off my flip-flops. "So I met Jolie," I say as Caleb sits down beside me. "She seems nice."

I know I shouldn't be asking him questions about Wesley, that it will only make me crazy, but I can't help myself.

He shrugs. "She is. I mean, I don't know her that well—I met her for the first time a few weeks ago when she came up to visit Wes."

"He's never mentioned her to me." I bury my toes in the sand. It's still warm from the sun.

"Really?" Caleb glances at me. "Hm. They've been together about a year. Wes was really bummed that he had to leave Portland. I think they're planning to apply to the same colleges next year."

Of course they are.

I pick up a handful of sand and let it run through my fingers. The thought of Wesley with this girl depresses me, which is totally ridiculous. Up until half an hour ago, all I wanted was to pay Wesley James back. And now—irony alert—he's found a new way to cause me pain and he doesn't even know it.

Unless he does.

Oh my God. I sit up, spilling sand all over my bare legs. What if Wesley knows exactly what he's doing? What if he's been shamelessly flirting with me these past few weeks, trying to get me to fall for him, just so he could rub his girlfriend in my face?

What if he's trying to get back at me for trying to get back at him?

"Are you okay, Quinn?" Caleb asks. "You seem a bit jittery."

"I'm fine."

I'm so not fine. Somehow, someway, Wesley James has learned about my plan. And he totally has a plan of his own.

Well, I am going to beat him at his own game. Er, at my own game. At whoever's game this is. Because there is no way I'm going to let him get the better of me.

Wesley James will not win.

As all of this is tossing around in my brain, Caleb is watching me closely. I turn to face him, hoping he thinks I'm still drunk and not having a psychotic break or something.

"You're sure?" he asks. "Maybe I should get you home."

I have to show Wesley that I don't care if he has a girl-friend, that the moment on the balcony meant nothing to me. And the best way to do that is right in front of me.

Caleb is the one I should want anyway. He's sweet and considerate and cute. He might not make me zing in the same way that Wesley does, but maybe that's not a bad thing. Maybe I don't need the zing.

So I lean forward and kiss him. And almost from the second his lips meet mine, I know it's a mistake.

It's not that kissing him is bad. It's just . . . nothing. I feel like I'm acting a part. I don't lose myself in the moment, the way I did with (ugh) Jason Cutler last semester. The way I imagine I could with Wesley.

But I keep going, hoping it will get better. Hoping that Caleb can make me forget all about Wesley.

fifteen.

"Make sure you come home right after your shift ends," Mom says, reaching into the fridge for a carton of juice. "I'll be calling to check up on you."

"Do you have to be so shout-y?" I hunch over my cereal bowl. She keeps telling me I'll feel better if I eat something, but really, I don't see how that's possible. I don't think I will feel well ever again.

Stupid beer.

"Some aspirin should take the edge off." Mom gives the empty-ish orange juice carton a shake and then sighs heavily, shooting me a dark look. "How many times," she mutters.

I'm lucky she's not madder about me coming home drunk

last night. I'm grounded for a week, but all that really means is I can't watch TV or use the computer.

"I haven't heard from your dad in a while," Mom says, pouring the dregs of the orange juice into a glass and sliding it in front of me. The sight of all that pulp floating on top of the juice is not doing anything good for my stomach.

I push the glass away. "He's been busy." Busy losing my life savings. But, of course, I don't say this out loud. Even after everything he's done, I'm still protecting my dad. Okay, yes, I'm protecting myself, too—if Mom finds out I gave him money, I'll be grounded indefinitely. But mostly I'm looking out for him. Or enabling him. Whatever.

Celia wanders into the kitchen in her bathrobe, her red hair completely hidden under a towel turban. She's been staying with us since we put the rest of Gran's stuff in storage. As much as I love Auntie C, I'll be glad when she's gone. She and Mom have been on me about visiting Gran, and holding them off is becoming harder and harder.

As if on cue, the two of them exchange a not-so-subtle glance. Mom clears her throat. "Sweetheart, we're going to see your grandmother this morning. I think it would be a good idea if you came with us."

"Mom, please. Not today, okay? I'm not feeling well. And besides, I have to work later."

"You have plenty of time before your shift starts," she says as Celia busies herself making coffee. "And it will be a quick visit. Gran gets tired easily, so we don't like to stay too long."

Maybe this is part of my punishment. She's going to force me to see Gran again.

"I'm not going."

The disappointment is clear on my mom's face and it takes a minute for her to respond. "Gran still has some lucid moments, Quinn. Not many, and not for long periods of time, but occasionally she's herself again." Mom accepts the mug that Celia holds out to her. "She's been asking for you."

My heart drops. The thought of Gran waiting for me, wondering where I am, should be enough to make me try. But I just don't think I can do it. I mean, what are the odds that she'll be lucid when I'm there? The alternative—facing that blank stare again—is way too upsetting.

Celia puts her arm around me. She smells like the vanilla bath gel we keep in the shower. "Quinn, sweetie, I know it's hard. But we want to make sure that you see Gran now. While she's still relatively well."

I squirm out from under her arm. "What does that mean?"

"It means that we need to be prepared," she says calmly. "We don't want you to regret it if something should happen to her. Your grandmother is old and the doctors aren't sure how much longer she—"

I back toward the door. I don't want to hear the rest of this conversation.

"Quinn," Mom says.

But I'm already gone.

sixteen.

"This is our big surprise?" I ask as a busted-looking white truck lumbers into the Tudor Tymes parking lot. I've been standing out back by the reeking Dumpster with the rest of the staff for the past five minutes, waiting for Joe's big reveal. "A food truck?"

To say I'm disappointed would be an understatement. I was hoping Joe was going to give us each a bonus—something that might help get me to London after all. I should have known better.

Wesley lifts his eye patch to get a better look. "Guess so."

I've seen food trucks all over the city, offering everything from Korean BBQ to gourmet burgers. And now, apparently, wholesome medieval fare.

"I don't get it," Amy says, crossing her arms. Her dark hair is divided into two neat plaits, more Bavarian milkmaid than member of the English court, but whatever. And while her costume is identical to mine—white corset laced over a blue velvet gown—she looks totally different in hers. But that's probably because she's pulled her corset down so low her nipples are practically showing.

Joe pulls the truck to a stop and hops out, smiling like a kid on Christmas morning. "What do you think?" He gestures to a sign tacked to the passenger-side door. "Tudor Tymes to Go!"

I'm not sure what reaction Joe was expecting, but we all sort of stare at him, silent, until the smile falls off his face.

"Food trucks are the new thing," he says, a bit indignantly. "People eat at the truck, they get a taste of how great our food is, they come to the restaurant. See?"

Not really. I mean, granted, I don't have a marketing degree, but I do know that we're a place known for our atmosphere. Our food? Not our selling point.

"We've got a corner on the market. There's no one out there serving anything similar." Joe rolls up the silver door on the side of the truck and motions for us to come forward. "I got it for a steal. Bankruptcy sale."

Now that I'm getting closer, I can just make out the ghost of letters on the side of the truck—Burger something—that Joe has partially covered with his makeshift sign. We all jostle to peer inside. And it's exactly what you'd expect a food truck to look like: a kitchen squeezed inside a truck.

"We're going to try her out downtown next week," Joe says. "So we need to start training this afternoon. Quinn and Amy, you're up first."

"Wait, what? We have to work in here?" For some reason it hadn't occurred to me that we'd be forced to work in the truck. Which, duh.

Joe frowns. "Who did you think was going to do it?"

Alrighty then. This summer is officially going down as the worst in history. Not only am I not going to London, but I have a very bad feeling that this truck is not air-conditioned. My velvet costume will not translate well in this heat and I will probably die of heatstroke. Which would perfectly cap off this whole rotten summer.

"Quinn, Amy, you're out here with me," Joe says. "The rest of you, back inside."

While everyone else files into the restaurant to start preparing for opening, Joe gestures for Amy and me to follow him. We climb up two narrow metal steps into the truck. It's really tight on space in here, crammed as it is with appliances and overflowing boxes of Tudor Tymes memorabilia, which clearly he's going to make us hock.

Joe's in the middle of giving us the grand tour when there's a rapid-fire knock on the side of the truck. A second later, a short, red-haired guy climbs the stairs.

"You're late," Joe barks at him as the guy squeezes his way inside. "Ladies, this is my nephew, Carter. He's going to manage Tudor Tymes to Go."

I know it's not fair to make snap judgments, but Carter kind of looks like he crawled out of a swamp. And by that I mean he's sort of dirty, with buggy eyes, and arms that are too long for his body. Definitely a guy you want to keep behind the scenes.

"While Carter is at the grill, you two will be serving customers." Joe points to the take-out window. "You have ninety seconds to get the food from order to customer."

Ninety seconds? There is no way. It takes us at least ten minutes to get a plate out at the restaurant.

"People have certain expectations about food trucks," Joe says, registering my skeptical expression. "They're on their lunch breaks, they want their food fast. So we need to give it to them as quickly as possible."

Joe shuffles around Amy to get to the fridge. "Most of the food will be preprepared, with the exception of the turkey legs—Carter, you'll need to fry those." He pulls open the dented refrigerator door. The shelves are empty except for industrial-sized jars of condiments. "Obviously, you'll be fully stocked when you leave here next week. If there's no lineup—and I don't think that will happen because we've got a real winning concept here—then you ladies will help Carter with prep."

"You mean, like, cut vegetables and stuff?" Amy says.

"Yes, Amy. That's exactly what I mean." Joe lets the fridge door slam shut. "Now, we've had to modify our menu a bit. We'll still serve turkey legs, of course, but also corn on the cob, salad, fries, and one of King Henry's favorites, rice pudding."

Joe spends a few minutes getting us familiar with the safety features of the truck, including pointing out where we can find the fire extinguisher (tucked underneath the counter) and the first aid kit (up front, in the glove compartment).

"What about the bathroom?" Amy asks. "I mean, there doesn't seem to be one."

"You're right," he says. "Bathroom breaks on your own time."

"But what if we really have to go?"

"You'll have to hold it."

"Well, what if we can't?"

Joe sighs and does what he always does when someone asks him a question he doesn't want to answer—he changes the subject. "In case someone comes by to check our permit, it's here"—he points to a small corkboard on the wall—"along with the truck's schedule for the next two weeks."

Amy and I lean forward to read the tiny spreadsheet. Pike

Place. Alki Beach. Rock Fest. We smile at each other. Maybe this won't be so bad.

I raise my hand.

"Yes, Quinn?" Joe says.

"Do we have to wear our costumes?"

Joe blinks. "Yes, Quinn. You have to wear your costumes." He says this like I've just asked the dumbest question ever.

"It's really hot in here." My costume is sticking to me.

"Yeah. There's no air-conditioning," Amy says. "Isn't that, like, against workers' rights or something?"

"I'll get you a fan." Joe moves on, showing us how to work the old-fashioned cash register, before sending Amy outside so we can role-play a customer interaction.

Amy skips up to the window and takes her time studying the menu board. "Hmmm . . . do you use partially hydrogenated oils in your fries? Because trans fats are really bad for you—"

"Amy," Joe barks. "Let's take this seriously, all right?"

Amy rolls her eyes. "Fine. I guess I'll have the special." She hands me her pretend-money, which I pretend-deposit into the cash register.

I call the order to Carter. He's leaning against the stove, studying his watch. When a minute passes, he hands me an empty plate.

I'm not sure how helpful this exercise is, considering we're not really doing anything real. I guess the test will come when we're actually out on the road. A prospect that seems ripe for disaster.

"Here you go!" I say with false cheer, passing an empty paper plate through the window to Amy. She eyeballs her non-existent order. I can tell she's thinking about complaining, but stops when Joe scowls at her.

He sets a tin can with a paper sign wrapped around it on the counter. He puts a couple of dollar bills in there—a trick that's supposed to encourage people to tip. "I'm going to leave you in Carter's hands for now," he says. "See you inside."

Amy smiles at Carter like she wouldn't mind being left in his hands. Which, ew. Amy is a flirt—she can't seem to help herself—and evidently swamp-monster looks and a boring personality aren't a problem, particularly if she thinks the guy can get her somewhere. Although I'm not sure where, exactly, she thinks Carter will get her.

Her attraction is short-lived, however, because he immediately power trips by putting us to work filling plastic squeeze bottles with ketchup from one of the giant drums in the fridge. He stands there, staring at us with his froggy eyes, while we try to keep ketchup from getting all over our hands.

When Amy's cell phone rings, she wipes her fingers on a paper towel and then grabs her phone out of her apron pocket.

Before she can even look at the screen, Carter snatches it away from her.

"No personal calls on work time," he says, dropping it into his chest pocket. "You can have this back at the end of your shift."

"What if it's an emergency?" she says.

"You can check your messages on your break."

I guess watching us fill squeeze bottles must be as boring as actually filling them, because Carter eventually steps outside. A few seconds later, a plume of cigarette smoke slips through the open take-out window.

"I don't know what I ever saw in him," Amy says.

seventeen.

The next morning, Erin picks me up in her Prius. Her saxophone case is on the backseat, buckled in like a baby. I dump my clarinet case on the floor and slide into the passenger seat.

"Mornin'," she says, handing me an iced coffee.

This, right here, is why Erin is my best friend. She instinctively knew how much I needed caffeine this morning. I didn't sleep well. I was way too busy obsessing about having to face Caleb at band practice today.

I've been hoping that Caleb and I could pretend like that night on the beach didn't exist. That he'd be okay with going back to being friends. But I've had, like, fifty text messages from him, and from the tone of them, I know that friendship is not what Caleb has in mind—his very dirty mind.

"So," Erin says, sending me a sympathetic glance. "Practice should be big-time awkward today."

"Yup."

"What are you going to say to Caleb?"

"Well . . ." I fiddle with my straw. "I was thinking I could tell him that I'm Amish."

Erin quietly digests my suggestion. "Like ride around in a horse and buggy, dress-like-a-Pilgrim, Amish?"

"I know, it's a bit crazy, but just listen." I sit up straight. "Amish girls are only allowed to date Amish boys, right? Otherwise their family kicks them out or throws rocks at them or something. Sooooo . . . if Caleb thinks I'm Amish, then there's no way that we can be together. At least, not unless he converts." I take a sip of my iced coffee, then almost spit it out as a thought occurs to me. "Oh my God. Do you think he'll convert for me?"

Erin sighs. "I don't think you have to worry about that. Considering there's no way he'll believe you're secretly Amish," she says, shaking her head. "Really, Quinn, you should just tell him the truth."

I roll my eyes. "Right. And what should I say? Caleb, I'm sorry, but the thought of ever kissing you again makes my stomach hurt?"

"Well, maybe you don't have to be quite that honest," she says. "But why not tell him that you like someone else?"

"I don't think that will make it any easier on him."

"Nothing is going to make it easier on him—or you. Breaking up with someone sucks."

"How can we be breaking up? We're not even going out," I say. At least, I don't think we are. "And besides, I don't like anyone else."

"Uh-huh." Erin turns into the school parking lot. There are only a few cars, but despite all the empty spaces, she pulls right up beside Wesley's truck. Just to make a point.

Wesley's inside, talking on his phone. He glances over at us and then glances away. Which is totally rude.

"Hm. Wonder what that's about," Erin says, unbuckling her seat belt.

"Oh, he's probably arranging to donate an organ to charity or raising money for underprivileged gorillas."

"Huh?"

"Never mind."

She shakes her head. "You really have him wrong. He's a good guy, Quinn."

"Again, you don't know him like I do," I say. "You're blinded by his stupidly handsome face."

"Ha! I knew you thought he was cute." She gets out of the car before I can debate this point, and opens the back door to grab her saxophone. "Maybe we should wait for him," she says.

"No way." I take one last long sip of my drink and then shove my empty cup in the cupholder. "Wesley is not going to make me late."

Besides, it's pretty clear from way he's deliberately not looking at us that he's not interested in company right now.

I climb out of the car and follow Erin into the school. I can feel Wesley's eyes on my back, but I don't turn around.

When we get to the band room, Erin has to nudge me through the door. Caleb's inside already and his face lights up when he sees me.

"Hey. I've been trying to call you," he says as I sit down beside him.

"Um, yeah. Sorry." I unlatch my clarinet case and busy myself with poking around inside so I don't have to look him in the eye. "I'm grounded. My mom wasn't happy when I came home less than sober the other night."

"Damn." He sighs. "Does this mean that you have to go right home after practice?"

And just like that, I have my excuse. I'll keep telling Caleb that I'm still grounded until he eventually gives up on me. Even if it takes my entire senior year.

It's genius. Much easier than pretending to be Amish. I don't know why I didn't think of it before.

I nod. "Afraid so. In fact, it'll be a long time before she lets me socialize again. A *long* time."

"That's okay," he says, putting his hand on my knee. "You're worth waiting for."

I smile tightly.

"Besides, we'll still see each other in band, right?" he adds. "At least we have that."

I make a move to cross my legs, so he has to pull his hand away. "Band. Yes."

Here's something I should have thought about before I let Caleb paw me: I have to sit beside him for the rest of the year. It's not like Mr. Aioki will let me move. We both play the clarinet. There's nowhere else for me to go.

WHAT WAS I THINKING?

I grab my clarinet and start to screw it together, cursing my bad judgment.

The band room door bangs open and Wesley trudges into the room. He's not smiling. As he makes his way down the row behind us, his tuba case bangs against the back of Caleb's chair. Caleb stiffens and turns around and shoots him a dirty look.

"Watch it, James," he growls.

????????

"Sorry, man. Not intentional." Wesley settles into his seat and drops his case in front of him.

"What's going on?" I ask Caleb.

His jaw tightens. "Ask James."

I haven't seen Wesley since the party. There's a dusting of blond stubble on his face and he has dark bags under his eyes. Looks like he didn't get much sleep last night, either.

"Dude, now's not the time, okay?" Wesley says warily.

Caleb snorts. "Right. You know all about timing, don't you, James?"

Clearly, these two are no longer friends. What I can't figure out is why.

Caleb puts his hand back on my knee. "By the way, I had a really great time the other night, Quinn." He's giving me this weird leering smile, like he's thinking about how we rolled around on the beach together. Blech. I wish I could scrub that memory from his brain—and mine, too.

Wesley looks away from us and starts to vigorously polish his tuba, his mouth set in a grim line. If I didn't know better, I'd think he was jealous.

Wait. Is he jealous? Because he has no right to be. He has a girlfriend!

I turn back around in my seat, thinking. I need to test this theory. I need to know if what almost happened between us at Travis's party was all in my imagination, or if Wesley really is into me. So instead of knocking Caleb's hand off my knee again, I lean into him. His fingers immediately slide up my leg, right below the line where my shorts meet my bare skin. I clamp my hand down over his, partly to see if this provokes any reaction from Wesley, but also to stop Caleb's fingers from wandering any farther.

I lean over to whisper something to Caleb, but really it's just an excuse to sneak a glance over his shoulder at Wesley.

"Maybe I can convince my mom to let me out this weekend," I say, just loud enough for Wesley to hear. His face is flushed. His breathing is all erratic, too, like he's working hard to keep his emotions in check.

Interesting.

I know that using Caleb to make Wesley jealous is wrong. So wrong. But it's also wrong to flirt with another girl when you have a girlfriend. It's wrong to stay with that girlfriend when you like someone else. And I think Wesley likes me. If I can prove that, well, then . . .

Well, then, what?

Okay, I haven't totally thought this plan through. But I'm going with it.

Caleb grins. "Yeah?" he says, nuzzling my neck with the tip of his nose. "Well, we should definitely get together then."

My phone beeps. I pull it out of my bag. It's Erin.

WTH?????

I look behind me at the brass section. She shakes her head slowly at me.

I widen my eyes, pretending not to understand her message.

She grimaces and begins to type. A second later, my phone beeps again.

What happened to telling him you're Amish?

I shield my phone so Caleb can't see the screen then type a quick message back to her.

Change of plans.

I don't have time to tell her about those plans, however, because Mr. Aioki steps up to the podium.

Wesley bolted out of the room as soon as practice ended, before I even started packing up my clarinet. He left without a word to any of us.

Seeing him miserable should make me happy—that's been my goal since the day he came back, after all. But it doesn't. Instead, I'm sad that he's upset, and also hugely guilty for dragging Caleb into this. I didn't consider his feelings at all.

I'm the worst.

On top of that, I promised myself that after practice today I'd tell Mr. Aioki I can't go to London, but I chickened out. I don't know what I'm waiting for. The longer I wait, the harder it will be.

I nestle my clarinet inside my case, half listening as Caleb and Erin chat about some indie movie they both want to see. I know she's dying to talk to me alone, but Caleb follows us out to the parking lot. Since he no longer has a vehicle, Erin offers him a ride home.

I'm surprised to see Wesley's truck still parked beside Erin's car. And I'm even more surprised to see him and Jolie standing beside it, talking. Or, rather, not talking. Wesley's staring at the ground. Jolie's scowling, her arms crossed tightly over her chest.

We have to walk past them to get to Erin's car. The closer we get, the harder my heart starts to pound. It's like walking into the middle of an electrical storm.

Wesley nods curtly at us, but he doesn't meet our eyes. Erin unlocks her car and we silently climb inside. Caleb gets into the backseat with Erin's saxophone.

"Woo, boy. Wouldn't want to be in James's shoes right now," he says as we pull away.

"What does that mean?" Erin says.

Caleb laughs. "Let's just say that he has a lot of explaining to do."

I catch a glimpse of Wesley in the side-view mirror, getting smaller and smaller as we drive away, and my stomach clenches as it occurs to me that his bad mood during practice might have had less to do with me and Caleb, and more to do with fighting with his girlfriend.

eighteen.

The tips of my fingers are orange. I've spent the last fifteen minutes chopping a whole mess of carrots into matchsticks so we can sprinkle them in the salad. I am sweaty and gross—the food truck still has no air-conditioning and there's no sign of that fan Joe promised. So the turkey legs aren't the only thing cooking in here today.

Also, Carter's hovering and, as I've discovered, he's a total perv. He keeps "accidentally" bumping into me, brushing parts of himself against me that I really don't want to have any contact with.

I'm about to "accidentally" chop off his fingers when the door swings open and Wesley enters.

The temperature suddenly goes up a few degrees. I'm stupidly happy to see him, until I remember that I'm not supposed to be happy to see him. I'm supposed to be avoiding him.

Carter's buggy eyes shift to the schedule tacked on the corkboard. "You're not Amy."

"That is true," Wesley says. "Amy needed the afternoon off. We switched shifts."

"You can't do that. We have a schedule," Carter says, shaking his head. "There are rules."

"I owed her a favor. And I didn't think it would be a problem. I mean, what does it matter as long as someone is here to cover the shift?"

What does it matter? It's a *rule*, clearly highlighted on page 19 in the staff orientation manual—no switching shifts unless approved by a supervisor. Seriously, has no one read the manual?

But we're twenty minutes from opening so there's not much Carter can do at this point. We won't get through the lunch rush without Wesley's help.

"You're also late," Carter says gruffly, handing him an apron.

"I had a bit of trouble finding you guys." Wesley ties the apron over his billowy white pirate shirt. He's wearing cargo shorts instead of the bottom half of his pirate costume, which, I have to admit, is kind of genius. All anyone can see of us from outside the truck is the top half anyway.

Carter barks at Wesley to help me finish the carrots. I push the huge, still half-full plastic bin toward him, mad that it didn't occur to me to wear shorts.

"Nice hairnet," Wesley says, grinning. Clearly, his good mood has returned.

"You're not going to think it's so funny in a minute." I smile back at him as Carter tosses a hairnet in his direction. Wesley acts like he's been passed a grenade.

"You're not serious," he says.

"You don't want to wear one, shave your head," Carter replies.

With a resigned sigh, Wesley pulls it on. It traps his messy blond hair, dips in a V across his forehead. It's almost impossible to look hot in a hairnet, but somehow Wesley James pulls it off. Damn him. Why does he have to be so good-looking?

"So why do you owe Amy a favor?"

"Oh. She found my swipe card." Wesley plucks a knife out of the knife block and studies my chopping technique, expecting, I guess, that I'll slow down and show him how it's done. I don't. I just keep chopping. "I guess I left it in the staff room. And I know I don't need to tell you about the rules."

He certainly doesn't. But the way he says it, it sounds like an insult.

Carter barks at us to hurry up, we're opening in five minutes. Helping us would be, well, helpful, but I guess that's not in his job description. He decides to step outside for a last-minute cigarette instead.

"What a douche." Wesley slows down on the chopping until I nudge him. We still have about a million carrots left and, like, no time.

"You're really not supposed to switch shifts," I say. "And anyway, he's just doing his job." Ugh. Why am I defending Carter, of all people?

An awkward silence descends. I've had some time to think about what happened at band practice—both the idiotic way I acted and Wesley's reaction. And I've reached the following conclusion: Making him jealous is stupid and a waste of time. If Wesley liked me—and I'm no longer convinced that he does—he is taken. And, really, even if he wasn't, it wouldn't matter. Because I cannot be with Wesley James. Not after what he did to break up my family.

We finish chopping the carrots, and Carter comes back inside and unlocks the take-out window. When he rolls up the steel door, all I can see for miles are people. An endlessly long line of people, all staring at us with hungry eyes.

"Yikes," Wesley says.

Yup. That about sums it up.

An hour later, the line looks like it's barely moved. More people keep coming. I guess Joe was right about having a corner on the medieval-food market. Maybe turkey legs *are* the next big thing.

Surprisingly, the three of us work pretty well as a team. We haven't come anywhere close to delivering the orders within the required ninety-second window—our best time, by my watch, was just over three minutes—but so far, no one has complained. Not even when we ran out of rice pudding.

After serving what seems like most of downtown Seattle, the lunch rush is finally over. Carter, Wesley, and I stare at one another in stunned silence.

I feel like we've come through a war. We looked directly into the face of a hungry mob and we lived to tell about it.

"I need a cigarette." Carter stumbles out of the truck, his fingers fumbling to untie his grease-stained apron. He can't seem to get it off fast enough.

"So that was fun," Wesley says, tossing his hairnet into the garbage can. He picks up the tip jar and starts sorting through the bills. "How much do you think we made?"

I don't even care. I'm too busy obsessing over how I will probably never get the fried turkey stench off me. Being locked in such a tiny space has magnified the stink. I am desperate to go home and take a shower, but we still have so much cleaning up ahead of us. It's like a bomb went off in here. Seriously, I do not even know where to start.

Wesley counts out the bills, smoothing them on the counter. "Two hundred bucks." He smiles at me, delighted, and he looks so much like the boy I used to know that I feel myself softening toward him again.

The feeling totally unnerves me. Every time I make up my mind to forget about Wesley, he throws me off balance. I fill the sink with water, while Wesley stuffs the money back into the tip jar.

"So . . . ," he says as I squirt lemon-scented dish soap under the running water. "What happened to you at the party? You sure left in a hurry."

I don't want him to know that my exit from the party had anything to do with him. Or his pixie girlfriend. "I wasn't feeling well. Caleb walked me home."

Wesley grabs a dishcloth and tries to corral the food crumbs covering the counter into a neat pile. "So you and Caleb, huh?"

I swallow. "Yeah. Me and Caleb." I don't sound convincing, but maybe I'm a better actress than I think because Wesley doesn't say anything.

Why isn't he saying anything?

He reaches past me to dump the crumbs into the garbage

can underneath the sink and his arm brushes against mine. It feels intentional and that makes it much worse.

"Q?"

"Yes?"

I glance at him and my heart starts to quicken. There isn't a lot of room inside this truck, but he's definitely standing a lot closer to me than he needs to. He's also staring at me with the same expression he was wearing at the party, when we were on the balcony. Right before he almost kissed me.

"I should have told you about Jolie," he says. "I don't know why I didn't."

I shake my head. "You don't owe me an explanation."

"It's just . . . I don't want any awkwardness between us," he says. "I really do want to be—"

I find myself holding my breath, hoping, against my better judgment, that he's not going to use the *F* word.

"—friends."

He's staring at my mouth when he says it.

What kind of twisted game is Wesley playing here? He's totally sending me mixed messages. This is all obviously part of a plan to get me to like him, so he can then . . .

Well, I haven't quite figured out his motive yet. But I know he has one.

I move away from him.

I start attacking the rice pudding pot with a scrub brush. A hunk of pudding skin hangs from the edge of the pot—so gross it actually makes me shudder—and rice is crusted onto the bottom, hard as cement.

Wesley takes the pot from me and he's standing really close to me again. Every nerve in my body is firing. This doesn't feel like friendship. This feels like so much more than that.

"There's something else," he says.

"Hello?" Someone raps on the counter. Wesley jerks around, and over his shoulder I see a homeless man standing at the take-out window.

"Argh, what can I get ye, matey?" Wesley says, leaning on the counter. "The turkey leg makes for a fine feast, if ye be lookin' for a hearty meal."

"Smells good," the man says, sticking his head inside the window. "Got any leftovers? Anything you were going to throw out?"

"No, but . . ." Wesley grabs the tip jar and extracts a five-dollar bill. "I do have enough for one special. Sound okay?"

The man smiles and Wesley sticks the bill into the cash register. He gives me a small shrug and then turns to throw a frozen turkey leg into the deep fryer. A cloud of hot steam instantly rises up, obscuring his face.

God, why does he have to be so nice? Why can't he be an

ass and shoo the guy away like Carter does? He's making it harder and harder for me to destroy him.

Wesley James may seem like he's a good guy—the kind of guy who feeds the homeless and builds houses or whatever for people in Mexico—but it's all an act. It has to be.

No one is that perfect.

And suddenly, I'm mad again. Angrier than I've been since the night Wesley first showed up at Tudor Tymes. Because he's a total fake. And everyone is falling for it.

Even me.

So while he's busy making lunch for Homeless Guy, I unpin the schedule from the corkboard. Wesley and I have only one shift together next week and it's at the restaurant. He never makes a copy of the schedule or writes down his shifts; he relies on his memory.

I check to make sure he's not paying attention and then I grab a purple feathered quill from the box of Tudor Tymes souvenirs that Joe is always pressuring us to sell.

The schedule is a photocopy—the original is posted in the staff room at the restaurant—so it shouldn't be hard for me to change Wesley's shift. Make him an hour late. Maybe two, for good measure.

Just enough to tarnish his suit of armor.

And, with any luck, finally get him fired.

nineteen.

Caleb's waiting for me at the entrance to the beach, a big wicker picnic basket hooked over his arm. He grins when he sees me, and while his smile doesn't go right through me the way Wesley's does, it does make me happy. I'm sure choosing Caleb is the right decision.

Pretty sure.

Mostly sure.

I mean, okay, I don't have the same crazy physical response when I'm with him that I do around Wesley, but you know what? Attraction is overrated. I may not want to rip Caleb's clothes off, but maybe that will come in time. He's funny, sensitive, and kind. And—as an added bonus—he isn't responsible for the destruction of my family.

"Hey, you," he says. He leans over to give me a kiss, but I turn my head at the last second. Instead of my lips, he gets a mouthful of my hair.

After what happened between us the last time we were on the beach, I know that there's a high probability of kissing in the forecast tonight. I'm hoping that this time there will be fireworks, that any lingering doubts about Caleb will be put to rest and he'll make me forget all about Wesley James.

So yes, my expectations for this date are high. Turning my head away when he tried to kiss me is probably not the best way to start it off. From here on out, I decide to be more open. If Caleb tries again, then I'm going to just go with it.

"Hi," I say. "You look nice."

And he does, if a little buttoned up. He's wearing navy shorts and a white golf shirt, with pristine brown leather sandals. His golden-brown hair is neatly parted, not a hair out of place. Not like Wesley's hair, which often looks as if it's never seen a comb.

Why am I thinking about Wesley again? I need to put him out of my mind, once and for all. He is taking up valuable space in my brain, space that should be devoted to this nice, available boy in front of me. A boy who has packed a picnic for me.

Caleb's smile widens. "Thanks. You too." He takes in my flowy blue sundress, his eyes resting briefly on my cleavage before traveling down the rest of my body. "Ready?"

I nod, kicking off my flip-flops. Caleb shifts the basket on his arm and reaches for my hand. I let him lead me through the soft sand to a quieter area of the beach. We don't speak as he spreads out a cozy plaid blanket on a patch of sand partially blocked off by a large piece of driftwood. I worry that we've run out of things to say to each other, five minutes into the date. The silence doesn't feel comfortable the way it does when I'm with Wesley.

Nothing with Caleb feels the way it does when I'm with Wesley. But I'm determined to change that.

We sit down and Caleb begins to unpack the picnic basket: roast beef sandwiches tightly sealed in plastic wrap, a bunch of red grapes, chocolate chip cookies the size of dinner plates. Two bottles of iced tea. I'm touched that he put so much thought into our date. And guilty that I haven't.

"This is great," I say, grabbing a cookie.

Caleb laughs. "Dessert first? My kind of girl," he says. He shifts, moving a little closer to me until his knee is touching mine. His skin is warm and tanned.

A picnic on the beach as the sun goes down—it's like something from a movie. It should be romantic. I should feel happy to be here with him. I *am* happy to be here with him.

Only why do I have to keep reminding myself of that?

I break off a piece of my cookie. "What happened with Wesley at band practice the other day?" I ask. I probably shouldn't probe Caleb about this, but maybe if we talk about it, then Wesley will finally vacate my brain. "I thought you guys were friends."

Caleb snorts. "That dude is no friend of mine," he says, shaking his head. "Clearly, he knows nothing about the bro code."

Bro code?

"You never go after a friend's girl," he says. "And being honest about his feelings does *not* make it honorable."

Wait, what? Is he referring to me? Is he telling me that Wesley has feelings for me? That I'm the reason they're no longer friends?

I think so.

Caleb's watching me closely, gauging my reaction. I'm trying very hard not to show any emotion, but my heart is jumping in my chest. I don't know how to process what he's just told me, what it means. And I don't have a chance to, because Caleb leans over and kisses me.

And it's not terrible. It's better than the last time. Nice enough that I let him push me back on the blanket. We make out, but I can't seem to let go and enjoy it because all I'm thinking about is Wesley. I'm obviously holding back and I guess Caleb senses that because after a few minutes he pulls away.

We lie on our backs, looking up at the sky. It's too early for stars, but I can see the ghost of the moon. The air between us has changed slightly, grown cooler by a few degrees.

Caleb is doing everything right. Any girl would be lucky to have him. But I'm not any girl. And he's not Wesley. And I can't do this.

I sit up, gathering my thoughts as I brush off the crumbs from the cookie I never got around to eating, crushed into a million pieces beneath us. I'm completely disgusted with myself for allowing things to go this far with Caleb, when I should have just listened to what my heart was telling me all along. I may not be able to have Wesley, but that doesn't make Caleb a consolation prize.

"What's the matter?" he says warily.

"This isn't going to work. I'm so sorry." I shift away from him. My first instinct, always, is to run, and I have to fight hard against that feeling now. But I owe it to Caleb not to.

His face darkens. "You're breaking up with me?"

I'm not sure we're actually breaking up, since we were technically never really together. Technically or not, though, I've obviously hurt him, and I feel like the worst person ever. I nod. "I'm sorry."

"Is this about Wesley?" A muscle in his jaw ticks.

I swallow. "Yes."

Caleb kneels and starts to chuck the food back into the picnic basket, muttering under his breath.

I'm making a complete mess of this. I have zero experience breaking someone's heart. It's awful, knowing that I'm responsible for the hurt on his face. I can only hope that one day he'll hate me a little less than he does at this moment.

"You know they'll get back together, right?" Caleb says. He stands up and yanks the blanket out from underneath me, sending sand flying everywhere. "They've broken up before. It never sticks."

I blink. "What are you talking about?"

He shakes his head. "What, you didn't know Wesley and Jolie broke up?" He laughs. "I guess the two of you are in for a fairy-tale ending."

"Caleb, really, I'm sorry. I just—"

"You know what, Quinn?" Caleb says. "I'm not interested." He gathers the blanket into an untidy bundle, picks up the picnic basket, and glares at me. "You two deserve each other."

Then he storms across the beach, leaving me with the sand and the sunset and a whole lot to think about.

I'm in my pj's, eating a huge slice of Aunt Celia's walnut cake when Mom gets home from work.

"What a night," she says, collapsing beside me on the couch.

She can say that again. I've been vacillating between feeling awful at how terribly I've treated Caleb and happy that Wesley and Jolie have broken up. And then to despair, because what difference does it make? It doesn't really change anything between Wesley and me.

Mom reaches over and swipes a bite of my cake. We've never talked about what happened the night of the Jameses' going away party, or what happened between her and dad afterward. But for the first time ever, I think I'm ready to.

"Did you know the Jameses are back in town?" I ask her. "I work with Wesley."

Her eyebrows lift. "I knew they were back—Celia mentioned he'd called—but I didn't realize you worked together. That must be nice for you. You two were such great friends."

I shake my head. "Not so great."

"What do you mean?"

Although I'd confided a little in Gran about Wesley, I'd never told my mom the truth about what happened between us. My dad is always a touchy subject. But if I'm going to move forward, if I'm ever going to forgive Wesley, then I have to clean out the wound.

"That night at the going away party, Wesley and I were hiding in the apple tree. We got into a fight about something"— I'm not about to tell her that we fought because I tried to kiss him and he backed away—"and I broke his magic wand."

"Okay . . ."

"Anyway, he got mad and he told on me."

She nods. "I remember that. I told him you'd buy him another wand out of your allowance."

"And he said not to bother. Then he said that he hoped Dad found another job soon. And when I asked him what he meant by that, he told us his mom mentioned Dad had been fired."

That was when I freaked out. Full on broke down. From the pained look on Wesley's face, it was evident that he didn't realize we didn't know, but the damage was done just the same.

That was the end of my family.

"Right." Mom looks confused. And I'm confused by her confusion.

"So if Wesley hadn't opened his big mouth and told you, then you wouldn't have ever known Dad was out of work. He could have gotten another job before you found out. You'd still be together."

Instead, the night of the party, my mom wouldn't even let Dad come back to the house to get his stuff. She packed it all up herself and sent it to Gran's. His entire life, crammed into two suitcases.

Mom's face softens. "Quinn, honey. That's not what happened."

"I was there, Mom. I remember it perfectly." All too well, in fact.

Mom sighs and I can see she's weighing her words. "Sweetheart, I already knew your dad had lost his job. He told me right before the party started."

Um, what?

"It wasn't the best timing. People were arriving and I was completely frazzled. But I guess he was worried it might come out that night, so he felt he had to tell me." She reaches for my hand. "It was the last straw. I told him I wanted a divorce before Wesley's family even arrived."

My stomach drops. I've spent years blaming Wesley for the demise of my parents' relationship, years believing that he's the reason we're not a family anymore. And it turns out that I've been punishing him for something he isn't even responsible for.

"Your dad and I had problems long before that night," Mom says. "He lied to me, for so long." Her face tightens and I realize that she's still a long way from forgiving him. So I guess I know where my issues with forgiveness come from. "Relationships are built on trust. Without that, you've got nothing."

She's right, of course. I couldn't let Dad be the villain— even though losing his job was 100 percent his fault—so instead I cast Wesley in the role. I've always been too willing to overlook my dad's shortcomings—and look where that's gotten me.

"So you can let Wesley off the hook now," Mom says.

I close my eyes. Letting him off the hook is the easy part. Fixing what I've broken is going to be much harder.

twenty.

Wesley flies into the restaurant, skidding to a stop in front of the hostess desk to say something to Rachel. Probably to thank her for calling him. According to my doctored schedule—the one that, until I arrived at work this afternoon, I forgot all about—he's not supposed to be here for another hour.

My heart pounds as he speed walks across the restaurant toward me, tucking his billowy shirt into his pants. His black boots are unlaced and the tongues flap against the leather.

I've had to cover his section—along with my own—for the past hellish hour. Definitely something I should have considered before I changed his schedule, but no less than I deserve.

"I don't know how this happened," Wesley says, following me into the kitchen. "I'm sure I was supposed to start at six."

"Really? Hm. That's weird."

He snaps his eye patch into place and then bends down to tie his shoelaces. "It doesn't make any sense," he says.

"Well, these things happen, right?"

Wesley glances up at me, his fingers stilling on the laces. He searches my face, like he's wondering about something, and my heart skips. He can't find out I was behind this.

He finishes doing up his boots. When he stands, I hand him a basket of bread.

"For table six," I say. "And watch out, they're supercranky."

This is true of most of the customers tonight, at least in Wesley's section. Because we've been short-staffed, everyone has had to wait longer for their food. And no one is happy about that.

Wesley takes a deep breath. "Sorry for the mix-up, Q. I know it's probably meant extra work for you."

He wouldn't be sorry if he knew I was behind it. In fact, he'd probably never speak to me again.

Before Wesley can deliver the bread, Joe pushes through the kitchen door. "Wesley. A word," he says. He turns on his heel and heads toward his office.

"What about my tables?" Wesley calls after him.

"Quinn can handle them."

Um, no. Quinn can't! Oh my God, I really don't want to go back out there and deal with table six.

Wesley smiles grimly at me. "Wish me luck," he says.

He's not going to need luck. It's not like they're going to actually fire him. Not for being late once.

But, half an hour later, I'm starting to worry. Wesley's still not back. The restaurant is full and table six has complained twice about the wait, even after I explained to them, as nicely as possible, that their orders are almost up.

I'm filling up their water goblets for the third time—seriously, these people are like camels—when Rachel tugs on my sleeve.

"You're needed in the kitchen," she whispers.

I shoot a nervous glance at the couple and their two kids, wondering if they've complained about me to Joe. "What for?"

"Staff meeting."

"Now?" I leave the water jug behind on the table and follow Rachel. "What's the meeting about?"

"No idea. Joe told me to gather everyone into the kitchen."

All the staff is crowded around the dishwashing station. Well, most of us anyway. Wesley's missing.

Wait . . . where is Wesley?

Joe waits until the dishwasher stops its rumbly cycle so we'll be able to hear him. "We all have customers waiting so I'll make this quick," he says. "Mr. James is no longer with us. He's been let go."

Wait, what? Wesley was fired because he was late, one time? According to the manual, three write-ups result in termination. Not one.

Oh my God. I did this. I actually got him fired.

Maybe it's all the steam back here or the smell of fried food, but I'm starting to feel really sweaty and light-headed.

"We've noticed that money has been going missing for the past few weeks. A lot of money," Joe says. "And we've traced it back to Mr. James."

Hold up. He thinks Wesley stole from the restaurant? Not possible. Wesley is a lot of things, but he's not a thief.

But no one says anything. No one rushes to his defense.

Should I say something?

"I realize this is a shock. It's a very unfortunate situation. We'll need to cover his shifts for the next week or so, until we can hire someone else, so if any of you are interested in picking up hours, let me know." And with that he stalks off.

Bruce shakes his head. "Okay, guys. Let's get back to work."

"I don't get it," I whisper to him as the rest of the staff files out the kitchen door. "Why does he think Wesley took the money?"

"It's probably the swipe cards," he says. Everyone is assigned a card on their first day and we use them whenever we need to place an order or get into the cash register. "It's actually kind of dumb of Wesley. The cards make it pretty easy to figure out if someone is stealing," he says.

Unless you're smart enough to use someone else's card.

I grab Amy when she comes back in the kitchen a few minutes later to drop off some dirty dishes.

"Hey, can I talk to you for a second?"

"Sure, I need a break," she says, blowing a piece of hair out of her eyes. "God, is it just me or is it really warm back here tonight?"

It's not just her. Maybe guilt makes you hot. Like you're burning in hellfire.

Or maybe the air-conditioning just isn't working back here.

I lead her out the back door, making sure that the brick is in place so we don't get locked out. The air out here is stuffy, but the Dumpster provides a bit of shade.

"So. What's up?" Amy says, perching on the picnic table. She fans herself with her hand and I notice her nails are painted dark blue.

There's no easy way to ask someone if they're a criminal, so I jump right in. "Did you have anything to do with Wesley getting fired?"

Amy's eyes narrow. "Why would you ask me that?"

"Bruce pointed out that all our transactions are tracked through our swipe cards."

"And?"

"And a few weeks ago you found Wesley's card. Remember?"

She stares at me. Ugh. She's going to make me spell it out.

"And . . . well. I'm wondering if you gave him the wrong one back," I say. "Maybe you gave him your card instead."

Amy hops off the picnic table and grabs my arm, pulling me farther behind the Dumpster so we're hidden from view. "Have you said anything about this to anyone?" Her fingers tighten.

"Ouch. God." I peel her fingers off and rub my arm. "No."

Not yet anyway.

Her shoulders relax. "All right, look. I wouldn't have had to do it if they paid us decently," she says. "It's, like, impossible to live on minimum wage. You have no idea. Besides, the restaurant can afford it. It's not a big deal."

Not a big deal? What is she talking about?

"Wesley was fired because of what you did," I say.

Amy wrinkles her nose. "I know. I do feel kind of bad

about that," she says. "But he doesn't need this job as badly as I do, so."

"That's not the point, Amy."

She gives me a hard look. "I'd appreciate it if you'd keep your mouth shut, Quinn. I really need to keep this job, as crappy as it is. I can barely afford rent. And there's no way I'm moving back in with my parents."

"You want me to cover for you?"

"You don't need to do anything. They already think Wesley took the money. Let them continue to believe that."

I feel bad about her situation. I do. But there's no way I can let Wesley take the fall for this.

"I need to get back inside." I try to step past Amy but she puts her hand on my chest to stop me.

She sighs. "I didn't want it to come to this, Quinn, but you should know: It's your word against mine," she says. "I don't want to throw you under the bus—I consider you a friend— but if I have to, I'll tell Joe that you stole my card and traded it with Wesley's."

I shake my head. "Why would he believe that?"

"Because," she says, smiling, "it's not exactly a secret that you and Wesley don't get along. Also? I saw you put a hair in that poor girl's food." She tsks. "Seems like Joe wouldn't be happy to hear about that."

Oh my God, Amy's the devil.

"You're blackmailing me?"

She shrugs. "Call it what you like. Just don't cross me." She gives me a little push and I stumble back. It gives her just enough time to get back inside, the door banging shut behind her.

"Here you go," Bruce says, sliding a Big Henry—basically a virgin piña colada—in front of me. "Maybe this will help."

I'm hunched over at one of the tables in front of the stage. The last customer left an hour ago, along with most of the staff, but I'm not ready to go home yet.

"Thanks."

Bruce climbs up on the stage to finish sweeping. The lights have been turned up and every corner of the restaurant is illuminated. The banners are threadbare, the wood on Henry's throne is badly in need of a polish, and I can see every dent in the suits of armor. Tudor Tymes might lose some of its magic when the lights are on, when every flaw is revealed, but somehow that just makes me love it more.

I'm hoping Wesley feels the same way about flaws. Because I've got plenty of them.

I'm not sure what to do about him. I have to get him his job back, but beyond telling Joe the truth and praying he believes me—and risk getting fired myself—I don't know what to do.

I'm halfway through my drink when Alan ambles over, carrying an overloaded turkey platter. He's still in full costume—blue velvet cape thrown over a burgundy-and-gold tunic. He's never not in costume, and he's usually the last to leave. If I didn't know better, I'd think he actually lived here.

I don't know much about Alan's personal life—actually, I don't know anything about his personal life, beyond that he used to do the weather on the local TV station.

"Pray tell, what's bothering you, fair maiden?" Alan settles himself heavily on the chair and tucks a paper napkin underneath his chin.

I sigh. "It's Wesley."

Alan nods. "Ah yes, young Wesley. I dare say, I did not think him capable of such an odious crime." His teeth rip into the turkey leg.

"Yeah, well. He didn't do it. He was framed," I say, trying not to show my revulsion at the flecks of meat collecting in Alan's beard. "Only I can't prove it."

Alan chews thoughtfully. "To stand falsely accused of something is a terrible thing," he says.

"So what should I do?" I sip at the dregs of my drink, feeling suddenly hopeful. Maybe Alan can help me.

He gnaws at his turkey leg again, pondering my question.

"My child, the answer lies within you. Look into your heart." He gives me a beatific smile.

That's it? That's his advice? Look into my heart? That is no help to me whatsoever.

And as I watch him wipe his greasy mouth on his napkin, I wonder how exactly I'm going to get myself out of this mess.

twenty-one.

Rachel shakes her head. "Wow, you really screwed things up," she says, leaning against the hostess desk. The thin leather strings that normally crisscross the bodice of her delicate yellow gown have been replaced with black-and-pink zebra-striped shoelaces.

"I know," I say.

"Like really badly."

"I know! Listen, are you going to help me or not?"

Rachel pinches her bottom lip between her fingers and studies me thoughtfully. "Getting Wesley fired is heinous," she says. "I wouldn't have pegged you as a backstabber."

My cheeks are on fire. Rachel's my friend and I hate that

this is what she thinks of me now. "Okay, I suck. All right?" I say. "But I didn't actually succeed. Amy did."

She narrows her eyes. "You got what you wanted, though. So what's changed? Why do you suddenly want him to have his job back?"

I glance away from her. "Because I like him," I say. So much my heart aches. Admitting this out loud to her somehow makes it even more real. "But more importantly, it's the right thing to do. He didn't steal anything."

Rachel nods. "Wellllll, I'm glad you've decided to use your powers for good and not evil, so okay. I'll help you. That wench Amy definitely deserves to go down."

"Thank you," I say, relieved. "Now help me figure out how to convince Joe to hire Wesley again."

"Throw yourself on his mercy." Rachel twirls a piece of her newly dyed blue hair. "It's worked for me a few times."

"No way. He'll fire me." This would obviously be no less than I deserve—Erin was totally right about karma—but honestly, I want to keep my job. I like working at Tudor Tymes. "There has to be another way."

And then Alan strolls past us. I remember our conversation last night and, like an answered prayer, an idea comes to me. Maybe he can help me after all.

I smile slowly. "I know exactly what we should do."

It doesn't take us long to convince Alan. His finely tuned sense of justice makes it impossible for him to turn us down.

Phase One of the plan involves getting Amy to come with me, which is harder than I thought it would be. "I just need to talk to you for one minute," I say, trailing her into the kitchen. I've been after her to come with me all night, but she's been avoiding me, which I guess isn't all that surprising.

Amy sighs heavily, dumping a load of dirty dishes onto the counter. "Fine, if it will get you off my back."

I walk away, but when I turn around a few steps later, she's not behind me. She's still standing in the same spot. "Why can't we just talk here?" she asks, her eyes narrowed in suspicion.

My heart begins to pound. She has to come with me for this to work. "Um, it's kind of a private matter," I say. "About Wesley."

His name gets her feet going; Amy hustles across the kitchen and grabs my arm hard, her fingers like a cuff around my bicep. She marches me down the hall, toward the staff room. The problem is, I need her over by the alcove.

I wrench my arm away from her. "Forget it," I say, walking quickly in the opposite direction.

"Oh no," Amy says. "You wanted to talk. Let's talk." Just

as I'd hoped, she follows me. I stop in front of the blue velvet curtain Rachel hung over the alcove to hide Alan, hoping Amy's too preoccupied to notice the big black boots sticking out from underneath it.

"I've been thinking about what you did to Wesley," I say. I need her to confess, to say that she's the one who stole the money, so Wesley can be vindicated.

Amy stares at me, her head cocked. "What are you talking about?"

My face burns. "You switched your swipe card with his."

I'm worried she's onto me, but then she says, "I already told you why I did that. Anyway, what difference does it make to you? I thought you hated him."

"That doesn't mean he deserved to be fired for something you did."

Amy leans closer and pokes me in the chest with her index finger. "Remember what I told you, Quinn," she hisses. "You better keep quiet, or I'll—"

She jumps back as Alan suddenly bursts through the curtain, his face thunderous. "What's this now?" he says. "Sir Wesley has been punished for your crimes?"

Amy shrinks as Alan towers over her. "No, no, Your Highness. You misunderstood."

He straightens even taller and puffs out his chest. "You dare to challenge the king?"

She shakes her head. "No, I'm not challenging you, I'm just—"

But Alan is well past the point of listening. He's already tried and convicted her, and is ready to mete out justice in the best way he knows how. "How now!" he booms. "Guard! Guard! There's a thief in our midst!"

Bruce appears from the shadows where he's been waiting. He shoots Amy a disgusted look, ready to lead her to Joe's office.

"It's not my fault," Amy begs, backing away from him. "Quinn! Quinn, tell him it's all just a misunderstanding! Please."

"But it's not a misunderstanding," I say coldly. "You stole the money and you let Wesley take the fall for it."

Amy glares at me. "Yeah? Well, you put a hair in a customer's food."

Rachel snorts. "Oh, please," she says. "We've all put hair in a customer's food."

Amy's face tightens. "Fine," she says, tearing off her Tudor Tymes apron and throwing it on the ground. She even grinds the heel of her boot into it. "I quit. I hated this job anyway." She storms past us and out the door. I wonder how long it will be before she remembers her purse is in the staff room.

Rachel cheers. "Good riddance," she says. She holds up her

phone, where she's recorded the entire conversation. "I'll go update Joe."

"Thanks," I say. "And thank you, Your Highness." I drop into a deep curtsey.

Alan smiles. "No need to thank me, Quinn," he says. "It was my pleasure. Now go tell Wesley he has his job back, if he wants it."

My heart falls. I've been so focused on trying to get Wesley his job back, thinking that if I could just fix this, then things could go back to normal. It didn't occur to me that he might not want to come back.

I need to find him and explain. I just hope he'll listen to me.

twenty-two.

Wesley's avoiding me. I've been trying to reach him for days to apologize. I even showed up at his house once, but I was too nervous to knock on the door.

Having Wesley shut me out has only reinforced how stupid I've been. About him, and about Gran. And while I can't do much more to fix things with him at the moment, at least not until he calls me back, I can do something about Gran.

So, finally, I am here.

I run my finger over the nameplate on the wall beside Gran's door. Her name is written in block letters on a sheet of card stock slipped inside a plastic sleeve. I guess they use paper instead of something more lasting because it's easier to change when the next resident arrives.

I don't like to think about what a new resident would mean for Gran. It's hard to believe that she won't ever leave this place. That this is her home now.

I'm glad that Celia insisted that she have her own room, despite it costing a lot more money. I'm happy we could do this for her, even though privacy probably doesn't top the list of things Gran cares about anymore.

I've been standing outside her door for a few minutes, trying to work up the guts to go inside. I told Celia and my mom that I was ready for this, but the reality of being here? So much harder than I imagined. Everything in me wants to run, to get as far away as possible, but I know I have to face what's happening behind this door. I owe it to Gran. And to myself.

So I knock.

Nothing.

Maybe she's sleeping? I knock louder. Still no answer.

A terrible thought occurs to me and my heart starts to pound. *Please please please let her just be sleeping. Please don't let me be too late.*

I take a deep breath and push open the door.

The lights are off and the curtains are drawn, but they're so thin the midday sun filters right through them, casting enough light that I can see Gran propped up in bed, a blanket pulled up to her chin. Her eyes are closed but they slowly flutter open when she hears me enter.

I sag with relief.

"Gran? It's me," I say. I sit down in the plastic chair beside her bed.

She's not wearing her glasses and it takes her a second to focus. I think I see a flicker of recognition in her blue eyes. I reach for her hand. It's knobby and warm and so familiar that it makes me want to bawl. I squeeze my eyes shut, to keep the tears from spilling over. I promised myself I wouldn't cry. Not in front of her. Not until I'm alone.

"Someone brought you flowers," I say, noticing the wilting tulips on her nightstand. Purple—her favorite color—arranged in a simple glass vase. The scarred wooden table is littered with tissues, a half-filled coffee mug, a small windup travel clock. So different from her nightstand at home, which was always stacked high with romance novels. Gran can't read anymore—she doesn't have the patience, but even if she did, I doubt she'd remember how.

I think that's the worst part of this disease. Everything Gran loved—her books, her house, her family—is lost to her. Just as she's lost to us.

Suddenly, Gran struggles to sit up. "Who are you? What are you doing in my room?" Her eyes widen in panic and confusion. It kills me to see her look at me like that. Like she's never seen me before. Like I am someone who could hurt her.

"It's okay, Gran. It's Quinn." I squeeze her hand. Maybe

there's something familiar about my fingers, too, because she relaxes and her eyes get this dreamy look.

"I have a granddaughter named Quinn," she says. "Do you know her?"

I nod. "We've met."

Gran reaches up and pulls the ruby hairpin out of her white dandelion-fluff hair, the one my granddad gave her when they got married, and presses it into my palm. The red, heart-shaped stone twinkles in my hand. "Could you give this to her? I've been saving it for her."

I lose the battle with the tears—they spill over my cheeks, fall like raindrops into my lap. "I'll make sure she gets it," I say.

Gran's eyelids are already starting to shut. She falls asleep quickly and I continue to watch her, the rhythmic rise and fall of her chest, remembering all the stories she told me about growing up in England. The story of her life.

I need to find a way to get to London. It may be too late for me to make enough money for the band trip, but I will start saving again, until I have enough to go. I will get there. And when I do, I will visit every place Gran has ever told me about. Maybe, if I'm lucky, I'll find something of her there.

I wipe the sleeve of my cardigan over my eyes. When I stand up to straighten her blanket, I hear someone enter the room.

I turn around and Wesley is standing in the doorway, holding a bunch of purple tulips. He's wearing khaki shorts and a black T-shirt, his normally wild blond hair tucked neatly behind his ears.

My heart swells. Happiness sweeps through me as my brain finally recognizes what my heart knew all along,

I love Wesley James.

How could I not have known that, all this time?

Unfortunately, if the grimace on Wesley's face is anything to go by, he doesn't feel the same way.

"I'll come back," he says, turning on his heel.

"Wes, wait."

He stops and looks at me warily. I can tell he's debating whether or not to just continue down the hall, so I jump in before he makes up his mind to leave.

"You haven't returned any of my calls," I say.

"Yeah, well. It took me a while, Quinn, but I finally got it," he says bitterly. "You'll never forgive me."

My stomach tightens. I have really made a mess of things. "There's nothing to forgive you for," I say. "Obviously, it's not your fault my parents got divorced. Blaming you for that was stupid. I'm sorry."

Wesley's fingers tighten on the bouquet and the flowers shake a little. "You got me fired."

I wince. He may not have called me back, but clearly he's

listened to my messages. I knew that the only way forward was to be honest with him about everything, even if he ended up hating me for it.

And it's pretty evident that he hates me.

"I got Amy fired, too, if that makes you feel any better," I say. "And I talked to Joe and he says the job is yours again if you want it."

Wesley shakes his head. "I don't know."

He's not reacting in the way I expected him to. I thought he'd be happy to have his job back. I thought . . . well, maybe I thought there was hope for us. Despite everything.

"I don't think I can work there anymore. Not with the way things are between us," he says. "I was hoping that we could be friends—"

Friends? Something breaks open in my heart. I don't want to be friends with Wesley. I want more than that. So much more.

"But I just don't see how that's possible now," he continues. "There's too much history. You can say you've forgiven me, but the truth is, Quinn, I'm not sure I forgive you."

The air is pushed out of my lungs. I feel like I'm underwater, a long, long way below the surface. I don't know how to make this up to him—I don't know if I ever can—and that's a difficult thing to have to live with.

Now I know exactly how Wesley felt.

"I'll quit Tudor Tymes," I say.

Wesley's eyebrows snap up toward his hairline. "What?"

"I'll quit," I repeat. "If working with me makes you uncomfortable, then I'll resign."

"So you want me to work there, without you?" His lips twitch, like he's fighting one of his trademark smirks. "You sure you aren't still trying to get back at me?"

Relief floods through me. Cracking jokes is a good sign. Maybe even a step toward actually becoming friends. And if all I can have from Wesley is his friendship, I guess I'll have to accept that. It will have to be enough.

"I'm done with trying to get back at you," I say. "I promise."

He nods. "Then I think we can handle working together," he says. "Although, I must admit, it was nice not to have to worry about being thrown in the stocks."

I smile.

Behind me, I hear Gran stir. I turn around. She's awake and she's watching us, a delighted expression on her face. For a moment, I think she recognizes us, but then the light goes out of her eyes again.

"Hi, Gran." Wesley walks over and removes the dying flowers from the vase on her bedside table, replacing them with the tulips in the bouquet he brought with him. "How are you today?"

Gran doesn't answer him, but she doesn't look afraid or

confused. And as Wesley chats with her about last night's base-ball game, I feel ashamed for ever trying to keep the two of them apart. It's going to take a while to forgive myself for that.

"I'll leave you two alone," I say.

Wesley glances over at me. "You don't have to go."

Yes, I do. I've already cost them time together. And maybe there are things that he wants to tell her that he can't say in front of anyone. Even me. Especially me.

"I need to get going," I say. "See you around?"

He smiles. "Seems you can't get rid of me."

Thank goodness.

I realize, as I'm walking down the hall, that being friends with Wesley is going to be hard—really hard. But not having him in my life at all? So much harder.

Later that afternoon, I'm wheeling my bike out of the garage when Dad walks up the driveway.

"I remember the first time you rode a bike," he says. "You were seven."

I roll my eyes. I'm not in any mood to take a trip down memory lane with him. I'm not in the mood for him at all, actually. I haven't seen him since our fateful breakfast when he told me he'd gambled away my money.

I stuff my bag into the white wicker basket attached to the

handlebars, then put up the kickstand and get onto my bike, prepared to ride right past him.

"Quinn, wait," he says. "Please."

I sigh. "What do you want, Dad?"

His hands are buried in his pockets and he's jingling his change, a nervous habit that used to drive my mom crazy. He glances uncertainly at the front door.

"No one's home," I say.

The jingling stops. "Okay, well, I just wanted to stop by to see how you are. And to bring you this." He pulls a check out of his pocket. I stare at it until he says, "Take it."

I reach for the check, my heart thumping. I don't give up hope easily, so when I unfold it and realize it's his child support payment and not the money he owes me, I'm disappointed all over again.

"It's not the full amount," he says. "Tell your mom I'll try to get the rest to her next week."

"Where did you get the money from?"

He shrugs. "I sold my baseball."

I blink at him. "Your Derek Jeter baseball? I can't believe you did that."

"It was just a ball," he says. "I didn't get much for it—not enough to give your mom what I owe her or to pay you back, unfortunately."

But it was all he had. And that counts for something.

"I'm sorry, ladybug. I was really hoping I could give you your money back in time for London," he says, his eyes getting misty. "I never should have taken it in the first place." He clears his throat. "I'm going to start going to meetings again. Today, in fact."

Right after my mom left him, Dad started going to Gamblers Anonymous, hoping it would win her back. But it was way too late. She wouldn't have anything to do with him. Once he realized that she was done, he gave up trying.

"Okay." I dig my keys out of my bag. I want to leave the check inside on the coffee table, where Mom will see it as soon as she gets back. "Do you want to come in?"

He hesitates. I can tell he's tempted to see the inside of the house where he once lived, probably hoping it hasn't changed, that something of him is still in there, but he says, "No. I'm good."

It's probably for the best. Because there's nothing left of him in our house. My mom made sure of that.

"Where are you off to?" he asks after I come back outside.

"I'm going over to Erin's," I say. I need to get her take on what happened with Wesley this morning.

There's no sign of Dad's car anywhere. He could have used the money from his baseball to get his car out of the impound. But he didn't. He used it to pay my mom what he owed her.

Maybe I'm letting him off the hook too easily, but that's the thing I'm learning about forgiveness; it's not something you just do for the other person, it's something you do for yourself.

"How about I walk you there?" he says.

"Sure," I reply.

We have a lot of ground to cover, far more than we can manage in the short walk to Erin's place, but it's a start.

twenty-three.

It's been six days since Alan sent anyone to the stocks.
Wesley's convinced it's because Alan's grown bored with it,
but I know the truth: He's in love. The proof is in the way he
can't stop smiling at Justine, the pretty brunette actress Joe
recently hired to play Anne Boleyn. Alan's also been wearing
his nicest royal clothes and he's trimmed his scraggly beard. I
think he's even lost a few pounds.

The best part? Justine always smiles when he's around, too.

Wesley's been back at work for a week. Things are better
between us. We're friendly. Friendly friends. It's fine.

Okay, it's not fine. It sucks, but there doesn't seem to be
much I can do about it. And while spending time with Wesley
is its own brand of torture, I can't seem to stop myself. We've

somehow fallen into the habit of carpooling to work together. He's giving me a ride home tonight, in fact, and my nerves are frayed because I've decided I'm finally going to give him Gran's letters. Hopefully, he won't be upset that I've hung on to them for so long.

The restaurant has just closed and I'm hurrying to clear my table before my shift ends when Wesley comes up behind me and pokes me in the lower back with a foam sword he borrowed from the gift shop.

"En garde!" he says.

I sigh. "That never gets old?"

"Nope."

"You're finished with your tables already?"

"Nope," he says with a grin. "But I could be done in ten minutes. Faster, if I had some help."

I roll my eyes. "I'll be right over."

I watch him head off to the other side of the restaurant, passing Rachel on his way.

"When are you guys just going to get it on already?" she says, plopping down in a chair and resting her elbows on the table. She's wearing thick tortoiseshell glasses, even though she has perfect vision. Fairly certain she bought them just to annoy Joe.

"It's not like that," I say, and I almost sound convincing. "We're just friends."

"Yeah, I don't buy it. I've seen the goo-goo eyes you two make at each other."

Maybe she thinks Wesley prodding me with a foam sword is flirting, when really, it's just Wesley being Wesley. He's like that with everyone.

"Rach, there's nothing going on between us," I say. My heart squeezes, because it's the truth and it's painful. And I guess Rachel can see that, because she reaches across the table and takes my hand.

"You want to come in?" I say as Wesley pulls his truck into my driveway.

He raises his eyebrows. "You're inviting me inside?"

He's surprised, I guess, because I haven't asked him in before. Usually, he just drops me off out front.

"There's something I need to give you. Something I should have given you a long time ago, actually."

Clearly, he's curious because he turns off his truck and follows me into the house. Mom's at work and Celia is out with friends, so we have the place to ourselves. Under other circumstances, this would be a great thing, but being home alone with a boy I'm really into, who isn't into me, just feels sad.

"Been a while since I've been here," Wesley says, poking his head into the living room. "Looks so different."

I nod. Mom redecorated after the divorce. New paint, new couch. New life. Took me a while to get used to it, but now I can barely remember how it was before.

My heart is pounding so hard I can hear it as I lead Wesley down the hall to my room. I push open my door and flick on the light.

"Well, well. Your room is still the same," he says. He walks over to the sepia-colored poster of Big Ben hanging over my bed, while I go into my closet and pull his letters out of the shoe box I brought home from Gran's.

I hold my breath as I hand him the stack, neatly tied together with a grosgrain ribbon. "I should have given these back to you a long time ago. I don't know why I didn't."

Wesley looks down at the letters. He runs a finger gently over the ribbon.

"I didn't read them," I say.

"It would have been okay if you had." He clears his throat. "I can't believe she kept them."

"Yeah, well. Gran's sentimental. She also never threw anything out. Ever," I say. "She had so much crap, Wes, you wouldn't believe—"

But I can tell he's not listening to me. His attention has suddenly shifted to something over my shoulder.

I freeze, quickly running through a mental list of all the embarrassing things I could have left out for him to discover.

Granny underwear? Tampons? But when I turn around, all I see is the Gruffalo balloon on my desk, slowly deflating.

Wesley brushes past me. He sets the letters on my desk and picks up the balloon, a strange expression crossing his features. "You saved it?" he says.

My face is on fire. Saving that balloon, well, it's basically a declaration of my feelings for him. And I'm pretty sure he knows it. "Oh, um. Yeah. I did."

Wesley's staring at me intently. The air between us is so charged, the hair on my arms is standing up. "Why?" he asks softly.

I swallow. This is it. The moment. I can continue to run. Or I can go for it.

But here's the thing: I'm tired of running. And really, I've got nothing left to lose. So I take a deep breath, and then I take the leap.

"Because you made it for me," I say.

Wesley covers the length of the room in less than a second. He pulls me toward him and kisses me, and he's such a crazy, blow-my-socks-right-off amazingly good kisser that I practically melt into the floor.

I can't even believe this is happening.

I am kissing Wesley James.

!!!!!!!!!!!!!!!!!!!!!!!

The balloon falls to the floor and my hands find their way

to his shaggy blond hair, which is even softer than I imagined it would be. Wesley's hands are sliding up my back, bringing me closer, until there's no space left between us. We are all over each other and there is nothing "nice" about it, no wondering if this is right or if I like him. There is no thinking at all, just fireworks.

Everything—*everything*—about this moment is perfect. And, like all the best things in life, absolutely worth waiting for.

"I knew you'd come around eventually," Wesley says with a goofy grin. We're standing at the front door and I'm trying to coax him out of the house before Mom or Celia get home. But he's making it *very* hard.

"Of course you did," I say, halfheartedly trying to untangle myself from his arms. "Really, Wes, you have to go."

He tightens his embrace and buries his face in my neck. "I like it when you call me Wes," he murmurs. Then he starts kissing my neck and all the resolve drains out of me. We start making out against the door and we don't stop until a pair of headlights shines through the window.

We quickly straighten our clothing and I run my fingers through my hair, hoping it's not totally obvious that we've been pawing each other.

Wesley sneaks in one last kiss, then takes a deep, calming breath and opens the door. Aunt Celia is standing on the other side, keys in one hand, a white bakery box in the other.

If she's surprised to see us, it doesn't register on her face. "You must be Wesley," she says. "I've heard a lot about you."

Wes shakes her hand. "All good things, I hope," he says.

She smiles. "All good things."

Not strictly true—unlike Mom, Celia knows I disliked Wesley for a very long time—but I'm glad she doesn't tell him that. No need to rehash the past.

"See you tomorrow, Q," he says.

I nod and close the door behind him. Tomorrow can't come soon enough.

I want to go to my room, where I can comb over every detail of the past hour in privacy, but Celia holds up the box and says, "I've got cannoli," so I follow her into the kitchen. Because who turns down cannoli?

"Your young man is very handsome," she says, cutting the string off the box.

My face flushes with happiness. My young man! "What are we celebrating?" I say, watching as she lifts out two perfect pastries and sets them onto the fancy floral plates we usually only use for special occasions.

She hands me one of the plates. "We sold Gran's house this afternoon," she says. "And your dad called me."

I pause, the cannoli halfway to my mouth. This is the first time Dad and Celia have spoken in months—it must have gone well if she's bringing home baked goods. Still, I'm stunned. "Why?"

"Well, he's been trying to reach me for a couple of days, but I've been avoiding him because I thought he wanted to talk about the house," she says. "I thought he was looking for money. And, as it turns out, he was. Just not for himself."

"I don't understand." Hope flickers inside me, but I'm afraid to get too excited, in case this conversation isn't going in the direction I think it is.

"Your dad told me that you gave him money and he gambled it away." She grimaces and closes her eyes briefly, but when she opens them again, she's smiling. "Quinn, honey, your gran would never want you to miss that trip," she says. "And neither do I."

And then Celia tells me that she's put aside some money from the sale of the house for my trip.

I squeal and grab her in a hug, getting cannoli cream in her hair. She doesn't seem to care, though, she just squeals and jumps along with me.

I'm going to London. I AM GOING TO LONDON!

epilogue.

LONDON, TWO MONTHS LATER

London, as it turns out, is everything that I expected it to be. And nothing like I expected it to be.

For one thing, the weather is crazy miserable—at least in November. I knew it would be dreary, but I'm used to dreary. Seattle totally rivals London for rainfall, so I was pretty sure I'd get plenty of use out of my Union Jack umbrella. And I definitely have.

It's the mist I didn't expect. It's thick and cold and settles over everything. It heads right for your bones, taking up residence until you don't think it's possible to be any colder, until warmth feels like a distant memory. In the short time I've been here, I've already discovered that the only thing that can get my blood circulating properly again is a hot bath. I've taken three in the past twenty-four hours, and I'm planning to have another when I get back to the hotel.

The crappy weather doesn't bother me. I don't mind the rain or the mist, or even the fact that, on the walk over here, I got splashed by a double-decker bus and the bottom half of my jeans are completely soaked. I'm way too happy to care.

Because London is the most amazing place. I feel like I'm trapped in the pages of a history book. Every building, every cobblestone street, holds part of the past. Gran's past.

I walk onto Westminster Bridge. It's still early, but there's already a rush of cars behind me. By the time I make it to the exact center of the bridge, the mist has started to lift. I can see the glowing round face of Big Ben across the Thames. I shiver, but it's not because of the weather. It's because I'm here.

Finally.

It was dark when I slipped out this morning, leaving Erin snoring, twisted up in her sheets. I should be in the hotel, too, catching some sleep with the rest of my jet-lagged bandmates, but I feel like I need to make every moment here count. Sleep is not part of my schedule.

Besides, I'll have plenty of time to catch up later, when I'm back at home. I need to pack a lot into the next seven days— more than I can possibly do in such a short span of time—and

I have to be focused. Although I'm already planning to come back next summer, after graduation, I want to make sure my first time in England includes all the places Gran told me about. Starting with this bridge.

The rain has let up enough that I can put my umbrella back inside my bag. I'm pretty sure I'm in the right spot—the place where my grandfather proposed, more than fifty years ago. The place, Gran used to say, where it all began.

I reach up and touch the ruby hairpin she gave me. Feels like she's here with me.

The night before I left, my family had dinner together for the first time in five years. My mom doesn't believe Dad's resolution to quit gambling will stick—she's been through it too many times with him already—but I'm happy he's trying. It's something. And I have to believe he means it. The alternative is just too sad to think about.

The sun is starting to paint the sky pink. I imagine my grandparents standing right here, looking out at the River Thames. Happy.

I dig my phone out of my pocket. This is a moment I definitely want to capture, so I can show Gran when I get back. I know she won't remember this bridge, or London, or even me. But that's why it's even more important that I remember it for her.

I'm lost in thought when I feel a pair of arms wrap around

me, drawing me back. I smile and burrow into Wesley's arms. "You got my text."

"I would have been here sooner but Mr. Aioki almost caught me sneaking out." He buries his face in my neck. His nose is cold, an ice cube against my skin, but he tightens his arms to keep me from bolting away from him.

He lifts the phone out of my hands. He turns me around, so our backs are to the railing, Big Ben rising behind us in the background.

Seattle is five thousand miles away—a million miles from where we started—and for once, I don't need to know what comes next. For once, I'm happy exactly where I am.

Wesley holds the camera an arm's length away and we squeeze together, as close as possible. And then he snaps the photo.

acknowledgments.

So many people are behind getting this book—and getting me—to this point. My name may be on the cover, but it's thanks in part to the time, love, and effort of many others, including:

Eric Brown, Nicky Darwin, Stella Leventoyannis Harvey, Abby Wener Herlin, James Leslie, Linda Quennec, Claire Sicherman, and Eljean Dodge Wilson—my wonderful writers group. Thank you for your support and encouragement through the years.

Kat Brzozowski and Holly West, two amazing editors—your keen insight has made this book infinitely better, and I'm so lucky to have had the opportunity to work with both of you. Lauren Scobell and the rest of the Swoon Reads team—thank you doesn't begin to capture it, but I'll say it anyway: thank you. The Swoon Reads community, for reading and rating this book and helping it get published.

All of my friends who cheered when I told them I had a book deal. Jennifer McKenzie, for a thousand years of friendship, advice, and support. Amanda James, the original "James" (although it must be said that you have definitely not ruined my life). Leiko Greaves, Pam Morrison, Stacie Palivos, and Katie Zachariou—I'm so grateful to have all of you in my corner.

My parents, Brian and Joy; my sister, Dallas; her husband, Todd, and their family; my in-laws, Jim and Jela Stanic.

My husband, Tony, for always believing I could. And my daughter, Lila, for being the best kid in the universe.

FEELING BOOKISH?

Turn the page for some

Swoonworthy **EXTRAS**

How to Make a Balloon Sword

Want to be like Wesley and impress your
friends with your mad balloon-twisting skills?
Blow them away with this balloon sword,
straight out of Tudor Tymes!

Supplies:

- 260Q twisting balloons (can usually be found in party supply stores)
- Balloon air pump (or the power of your own lungs)

Steps:

1. Inflate a balloon and tie a knot in the end.
2. Create the handle of the sword by folding one end of the balloon, making a loop just big enough to get your hand through.

3. Twist the two sections at the bottom of the loop together three times to secure.

4. Push the end of the balloon through the loop handle.

5. Pull the "blade" of the sword straight.

A Coffee Date

with author Jennifer Honeybourn
and her editor, Holly West

"Getting to Know You"

Holly West (HW): What was the first romance novel you ever read?

Jennifer Honeybourn (JH): I've always been a big reader, so I can't remember exactly what the first romance novel I ever read was, but Susan Elizabeth Phillips made a big impact on me when I was a teenager. I loved her books. (Still do.)

HW: Who is your OTP, your favorite fictional couple?

JH: I would have to say Anna Oliphant and Etienne St. Clair from *Anna and the French Kiss* by Stephanie Perkins. I love love love both of those characters! But a very close second would be Veronica Mars and Logan Echolls.

HW: Do you have any hobbies? Other than writing, of course. I don't think writing counts as a hobby when you are a published author.

JH: Reading. I would almost rather read than do anything

else in life. There is nothing like getting lost in a really great book.

HW: In *Wesley James Ruined My Life*, Quinn dreams of visiting England. If you could go anywhere in the world, where would you visit?

JH: So many places! I'd like to go back to Europe; there are a lot of countries there I have yet to see. I would also love to road trip through the southern U.S. And I am *dying* to go to the Wizarding World of Harry Potter in Florida.

HW: And my favorite question, if you were a superhero, what would your superpower be?

JH: Probably time manipulation. It would be great to speed up time when I'm really impatient (like commuting in heavy traffic) or slow it down when something great is happening, like extending a moment you don't want to end.

"The Swoon Reads Experience"

HW: How did you first learn about Swoon Reads?

JH: I came across Swoon Reads on Twitter, actually. I was following a bunch of literary agents and one of them retweeted Katy Upperman's announcement for her book, *Kissing Max Holden*. Katy's book was chosen by Swoon Reads, and I found the crowdsourcing model of discovering new books really interesting and exciting.

HW: What made you decide to post your manuscript?

JH: Well, as I write YA romance, I felt like my book might be a good fit with the Swoon Reads imprint. I don't have an agent and the doors to traditional publishing are usually closed without one, so I really appreciated the opportunity to submit my book directly. I also loved that I would have the chance to get reader feedback on my manuscript.

HW: What was your experience like on the site before you were chosen?

JH: Posting on Swoon Reads was such a great experience. It's a very supportive, positive community. And I really liked how Swoon Reads involved the readers, whether it's through rating and commenting on manuscripts or voting on cover designs. Working with the Swoon Reads team behind the scenes has been just as wonderful. I feel incredibly lucky to be part of it all.

HW: Once you were chosen, who was the first person you told and how did you celebrate?

JH: I told my husband and daughter. I may have jumped up and down a little (or a lot). Publishing a book has been something

I've dreamed about my entire life, so I'm still wrapping my head around it (and still pinching myself).

HW: When did you realize you wanted to be a writer?

JH: I think I was in the second grade. I've been writing off and on since then, but it's only been in the past six years or so that I've dedicated myself to writing YA.

HW: Do you have any writing rituals?

JH: Not any rituals, really, but I do write on my phone quite a bit. Sometimes when life gets busy, I have to sneak writing in whenever and wherever possible and that often means ten or fifteen minutes on my phone. I can get a surprising amount done in those ten or fifteen minutes, if I need to.

HW: Where did the idea for *Wesley James Ruined My Life* start?

JH: I went to a Renaissance Faire a few years ago. I loved the atmosphere, the idea that these people participating in the Faire were so committed to dressing and acting like they were living in England five hundred years ago. I thought it would make a great setting for a book. And I wanted to write about two people who have feelings for each other, but who sometimes rub each other the wrong way, sort of in the vein of Sam and Diane from *Cheers*. (I know, I know! This totally dates me, but what can I say. I grew up in the eighties.)

HW: Do you ever get writer's block? How do you get back on track?

JH: I don't really get writer's block, at least not for a long period of time. I think it's because I write in my day job, so I'm used to deadlines and just getting it done. If I'm struggling with a scene, it often helps if I step away and move on to another part of the story and then go back to that scene later. Some days, if I'm tired or just not feeling creative, I take a walk or focus on something else and that usually helps me recharge.

HW: What's the best writing advice you've ever heard?

JH: Write what you want to read. I love YA books, so that's what I write. I've tried to write in other genres, but nothing gets me as excited or seems to fit my voice as well as YA.

"The Swoon Index"

HW: On the site we have something called the Swoon Index where readers can share the amount of Heat, Laughter, Tears, and Thrills in each manuscript. Can you tell me something (or someone!) that always turns up the heat?

JH: A really well-written kissing scene! Jenn Bennett does love scenes very well in *The Anatomical Shape of a Heart* (one of my favorite books).

HW: What always makes you laugh?
JH: My daughter. She's a naturally funny kid. Oh, and Ricky Gervais in the British version of *The Office*. British humor in general, actually.

HW: Makes you cry?
JH: *Love You Forever* by Robert Munsch. That book, I can't get through it without crying. And the movie *Beaches* destroys me every time.

HW: Sets your heart pumping?
JH: Anything that makes me feel connected to the world or another person—usually it's something creative, like through a book, a movie, or a play.

HW: And finally, tell us all what makes you swoon!
JH: Happy endings!

Wesley James
Ruined My LIFE

Discussion Questions

1. When the novel opens, Quinn is reintroduced to Wesley James, whom she hasn't seen in five years. What does Quinn's reaction to Wesley tell you about her?

2. If you worked at Tudor Tymes, what character in King Henry's court would you play and why? What would your costume look like?

3. How would you describe the two main characters, Quinn and Wesley? How do they differ from each other? Do they have any common personality traits?

4. *Wesley James Ruined My Life* is told from Quinn's perspective. How might the novel be different if it were told from Wesley's perspective instead?

5. How would you describe Quinn's family? How do you think her relationship with her parents—and her parents'

relationship with each other—informs her view of the world?

6. How does Quinn's relationship with her grandmother shape her feelings about Wesley James?

7. Forgiveness is a theme in *Wesley James Ruined My Life*. Why do you think it was so difficult for Quinn to forgive Wesley?

8. How does Quinn change over the course of the novel?

9. For Quinn and Wesley, the children's book *The Gruffalo* played a role in bringing them together. What book has had an impact on your life? Why?

10. What does going to England represent for Quinn?

From the author of *How to Say I Love You Out Loud*
comes a novel that proves everyone
deserves a second chance.

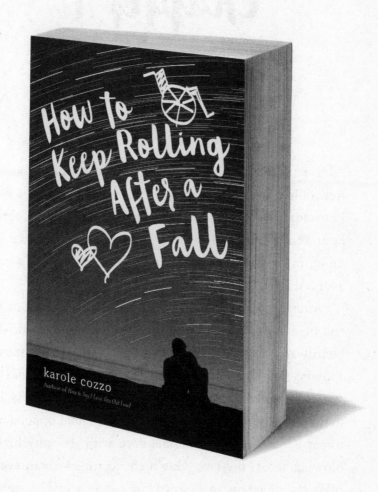

Keep reading for a sneak peek.

Chapter 1

As I park in the lot of the Harborview Nursing and Rehabilitation Center, I realize that, for the first time ever, I'm actually excited to be there. I'm working a short, three-hour shift, and the shift itself won't be so bad, since I'm filling in on the orthopedics wing, where Jeremiah's been assigned.

After work, the two of us have plans to check out the end-of-summer party that spans the length of Ocean Isle's boardwalk. Since I've seen it in those mailers that started showing up after the Fourth of July, the phrase *end-of-summer* has stirred feelings of anxiety, loss, and sadness. But tonight it means it's time for a party. One final opportunity to eat handfuls of hot caramel corn with the salty breeze blowing across my face. One night to forget about everything else going on, in a crowd large and chaotic enough to get lost in.

I lift my butt off the seat and scrunch my hair as I look in the rearview mirror. Once upon a time, I was a shoo-in for "Best Hair" in the senior superlatives—it's long and wildly curly, with natural highlights. All summer long I've tucked it under a baseball cap with the brim pulled down anytime I've been forced to leave my house. But not tonight. I made an effort to look good for Jeremiah. And I want to pretend I'm the girl I used to be.

Walking across the parking lot, I decide this place would be a lot more appealing if there was, you know, an *actual* view of the harbor. Instead, it's located miles inland, in the middle of a bleak field. The builders tried to spruce it up with the usual gazebos and flower beds, but the name is still a bold-faced lie. It's a depressing place to be, for all of us who are here because we have no choice in the matter.

But not tonight! I think, breezing through the automatic doors with renewed energy as I picture Jeremiah's face. *Tonight, it's a good place to be.* I head toward the nurses' station to clock in, but when I catch a glimpse of Jeremiah through the glass-paneled cafeteria walls, I make a detour, a sudden diet Dr Pepper craving developing.

I feel giddy as I walk in his direction. We've been flirting for the past two weeks, since I started my stint at the rehab center. Jeremiah's a sophomore at Rutgers University, with a long-term plan for med school and a specialty in orthopedics—as he explained it to me, "I want to break some bones and fix 'em up again." Jeremiah's got it all worked out, but his plans are on hold at the moment. He's taking a semester off to help out with some family issues. He hasn't said what kind of issues, and I haven't felt right asking; I assume he'll tell me eventually.

In the meantime, I'm content with the flirting. Jeremiah's really hot—Abercrombie model hot, with the cool hair, and the scruff, and the smirk. He even looks good in scrubs. "One day women are going to be falling down the stairs on purpose just to end up in your waiting room," I've teased him.

He's sweet, too, taking the mop out of my hands and pushing it himself, and one time walking me to my car under an umbrella from the lost and found when it started pouring without warning. Then two nights ago, he snatched my phone and programmed his number. "So call me tonight," he'd said all coolly as he tossed it back. I had, and now we have a date.

Jeremiah turns away from the register and slides his wallet into the back pocket of his scrubs, and his eyes meet mine. I smile and wave and wait for him to smile back.

But he doesn't smile. He glowers instead, his brown eyes ignited with a fury that turns them amber.

"I know who you are." He's not discreet; he's loud, pointing his index finger in my direction. "And you can go straight to hell."

The blood drains from my face and runs cold. I want to vanish, but I can't move. My feet feel as if they're stuck in the wet sand left behind when a wave recedes, weighted down and useless.

A few trays clatter against steel, and then the room is deathly quiet. Workers stop serving, midscoops of mashed potatoes. Residents stop talking. The scene unfolds before me in slow motion as people who have had strokes and people in wheelchairs struggle to turn their heads in my direction.

"Nice try, *Nicole*." He says my full name, the one I'd used to introduce myself, like an accusation. "Nikki Baylor, right? I know who you are. You forgot your ID badge yesterday. Now let me tell you who *I* am." Jeremiah approaches and thrusts his right hand toward me with such force it jams against my rib cage. It's almost a shove. "Jeremiah Jordan. Taylor Jordan's my sister. My baby sister, for that matter."

I hang my head and clench my fists at the same time, the mention of her name evoking the usual combination of shame and regret and a desire to run and hide. Except my feet are still stuck in the damn sand.

He folds his arms across his chest. "Guess it's my bad. You should really find out a person's last name before asking her out." Jeremiah doesn't say anything else and I look up, but it turns out he was saving one final zinger. "But now I know. And now it makes me sick to look at your face."

Tears form in my eyes at once. It sort of makes me sick to look at my face now, too, but Jeremiah had changed that for a few weeks. Before I actually start crying, thankfully, whatever's holding me in place loosens and I run from the room. I dart through the side door and into the central courtyard, the late-afternoon sun glaring down on me like the harsh lights inside the questioning room of the police station.

I choke back my tears, bending over and grabbing on to

my knees for support. I'll never escape this. This is going to follow me forever. I can pretend to be someone I'm not—I can pretend to be the person I *used* to be—but it's nothing more than playing a part.

I shake my head back and forth and wipe my eyes with the back of my hand, struggling to wrap my head around what just happened, feeling like I have whiplash. Jeremiah had come and gone so fast. The prospect of happiness had been so fleeting. I walked in the door envisioning the warmth of his smile; now all I can remember is the cold hatred in his eyes.

What the hell just happened?

"That was pretty harsh."

I straighten and turn around . . . then look down. The boy is in a wheelchair more lightweight than most I see around here, and he can't be much older than me. But he has a more mature look about him, something about his deep-set hazel eyes and square jaw that makes him look more like a young man and less like a boy. His light-brown hair falls to his chin, and the muscular build of his upper body makes me think he might've been a badass at one point.

I square my shoulders and lift my chin. "I probably deserve it."

"Highly doubt that." He wheels a bit closer, shaking his head. "That was a bad scene back there."

"Well, you don't know what you're talking about." I stare into the distance and blow out the breath I realize I've been holding. "If you did, you probably would've stood up and applauded him."

"Nah, I don't think so." A hint of a smile plays on his bow-shaped lips.

"Trust me, you would've."

"No, I don't think so," he repeats. He taps his knuckles against the wheels of his chair. "Standing ovations, not really my thing."

I cringe and want to die. "Oh my God. I'm really sorry."

"No apology necessary. I'm not easily offended."

"Still. I'm sorry."

He nods once in acknowledgment. "'S okay." Then he tilts his head and studies me. "Anyway, I've seen you around here a couple of times. And I think you have a really nice face. I have a hard time figuring why it makes that dude want to puke."

I smile in spite of everything, just for a second. Then reality sets in again, and I cover my eyes with my hand. "Today officially sucks. And I need to clock in. Like, five minutes ago." I take a deep breath, trying to imagine how I can possibly make myself go back inside. "But I can't go back in there."

Check out more books chosen for publication by readers like you.